PLOUGHSHARES

Winter 1993-94 · Vol. 19, No. 4

GUEST EDITORS
Russell Banks and Chase Twichell

EXECUTIVE DIRECTOR
DeWitt Henry

MANAGING EDITOR & FICTION EDITOR
Don Lee

POETRY EDITOR
David Daniel

ASSISTANT EDITOR
Jessica Dineen

FOUNDING PUBLISHER
Peter O'Malley

ADVISORY EDITORS

Russell Banks
Anne Bernays
Frank Bidart
Rosellen Brown
James Carroll
Madeline DeFrees
Rita Dove
Andre Dubus
Carolyn Forché
George Garrett
Lorrie Goldensohn
David Gullette
Marilyn Hacker
Donald Hall
Paul Hannigan
Stratis Haviaras
Fanny Howe

Marie Howe
Justin Kaplan
Bill Knott
Maxine Kumin
Philip Levine
Thomas Lux
Gail Mazur
James Alan McPherson
Leonard Michaels
Sue Miller
Jay Neugeboren
Tim O'Brien
Joyce Peseroff
Jayne Anne Phillips
Robert Pinsky
James Randall
Alberto Alvaro Ríos

M. L. Rosenthal
Lloyd Schwartz
Jane Shore
Charles Simic
Maura Stanton
Gerald Stern
Christopher Tilghman
Richard Tillinghast
Chase Twichell
Fred Viebahn
Ellen Bryant Voigt
Dan Wakefield
Derek Walcott
James Welch
Alan Williamson
Tobias Wolff
Al Young

PLOUGHSHARES, a journal of new writing, is guest-edited serially by prominent writers who explore different and personal visions, aesthetics, and literary circles. PLOUGHSHARES is published in April, August, and December at Emerson College, 100 Beacon Street, Boston, MA 02116-1596. Telephone: (617) 578-8753. Phone-a-Poem: (617) 578-8754.

SUBSCRIPTIONS (ISSN 0048-4474): $19/domestic and $24/international for individuals; $22/domestic and $27/international for institutions. See last page for order form.

UPCOMING: Spring 1994, Vol. 20, No. 1, a poetry and fiction issue edited by James Welch, will appear in April 1994 (editorially complete). Fall 1994, Vol. 20, Nos. 2 & 3, a special issue of personal narratives edited by Rosellen Brown, will appear in August 1994.

SUBMISSIONS: Please see back of issue for detailed submission policies.

BACK ISSUES are available from the publisher. Write or call for abstracts and a price list. Microfilms of back issues may be obtained from University Microfilms. PLOUGHSHARES is also available as a CD-ROM full-text product from UMI and Information Access Company. INDEXED in M.L.A. Bibliography, American Humanities Index, Index of American Periodical Verse, Book Review Index. Self-index through Volume 6 available from the publisher; annual supplements appear in the fourth number of each subsequent volume. All rights for individual works revert to the authors upon publication.

DISTRIBUTED by Bernhard DeBoer (113 E. Centre St., Nutley, NJ 07110), Fine Print Distributors (6448 Highway 290 East, Austin, TX 78723), Ingram Periodicals (1226 Heil Quaker Blvd., La Vergne, TN 37086), Inland Book Co. (140 Commerce St., East Haven, CT 06523), and L-S Distributors (130 East Grand Ave., South San Francisco, CA 94080). PRINTED by Edwards Brothers.

PLOUGHSHARES receives additional support from the National Endowment for the Arts, the Lannan Foundation, and the Massachusetts Cultural Council. Major new marketing initiatives have been made possible by the Lila Wallace–Reader's Digest Literary Publishers Marketing Development Program, funded through a grant to the Council of Literary Magazines and Presses. The opinions expressed in this magazine do not necessarily reflect those of Emerson College, the editors, the staff, the trustees, or the supporting organizations.

CONTENTS

Ploughshares · Winter 1993-94

Strictly in the Interests of Plausibility

I like thinking of the painting chosen for the cover of this issue as a visual representation of our theme of *Borderlands*. The artist, A. Artidor, is Haitian, contemporary, and not very well-known. My co-editor and I came across it in a Haitian art gallery on the island of Guadeloupe. It is a small (16" x 18") oil on masonite, and its more or less realistic representation of historical subject matter is typical of one of several groups of younger artists from Cap-Haitien.

The painting is skillfully executed—it appears to accomplish exactly what the artist set out to accomplish. The colors, although bright and lavish, are nonetheless delicate and precisely arranged, laid down entirely and pointedly without shadow under the savage noontime Caribbean sun, suggesting that the painting could not have been made by an artist who had not lived in the harsh light of the New World—or, let us say, the non-European world. And had not experienced its stark unromantic darkness as well, for it is a narrative, the one in which everyone steps on his own shadow—a Haitian High Noon.

The painting dramatizes a particularly poignant, even if briefly triumphant, moment in the history of the European enslavement of Africans in the Americas. The perspective, the narrative point of view, is that of a modern Haitian descendent of slaves. His portrayal of a single moment in time, Toussaint L'Ouverture's acceptance of Napoleon's first diplomatic representatives to a newly independent Haiti alludes, like a good Chekhovian short story, to an unspeakable time past and a horrifying, bitter time to come. It is unsentimental, ironic, and morally exact.

The victorious ex-slave Toussaint and his empress are portrayed not as heroic, god-like figures out of African (or Roman, Napoleonic, or Washingtonian) mythology, but as mere mortals standing at last on a level plane with the temporarily defeated Europeans, who, despite their past crimes, are pictured as no less mortal than they. The physical scene is native to the Americas—cacti, mountains, tropical forest, Caribbean sky—but the figures are wearing the costumes of late eighteenth-century European aristocrats, and they are all clearly aware of the momentousness of the occasion and are trying, not without a little stiffness, to play their appropriate roles.

There is a sad, brilliant symmetry to the painting—the African man and woman particularized in all their humanity (I especially like Toussaint's sideburns), and facing them the pair of European men, equally particularized, equally human; the elaborate Parisian tailoring, ruffles, bustles, and epaulets on the four figures, and the bare, ruined plantation on which they stand; the reversal of political conventions, in which for the first time white Europeans are requesting recognition from black Americans (by means of documents written in French, however), and the persistence of ancient diplomatic forms and niceties; the angelic blue sky above and the demonic land below, and the four poor, forked creatures between. It is a purely democratic moment specific to the imagination of those Americans (north, south, and meso-) whose history has been most characterized by powerlessness and oppression, and it has been captured by the artist with humor, compassion, and profound sadness. From his height in Cap-Haitien, he stands on a borderland, looks both ways in time, and it is as if he sees too much.

These, then, are the qualities that I have looked for among the hundreds of fiction manuscripts generously submitted for this issue of *Ploughshares*. Are they aesthetic qualities? one might ask. Or political? The answer, of course, is neither and both. Increasingly, however, in recent years I have found it difficult to generate much affection for fiction that portrays American society and history as monoracial, monocultural, and monolingual, with no significant gender or class barriers. Fiction that gives the lie to life. Simply, it has no plausibility for me, even though I myself am a white Protestant middle-class heterosexual male. In search of plausibility, then, if not the simple truth, I have been drawn more and more to fiction by writers who see themselves as situated in a society that puts every American man and woman on the borders of race, culture, language, gender, and class, and who view their world not from the privileged center of their own private Idaho, but from out there on the edges, where they are obliged to look both ways, as if at a dangerous crossing, and say what they see coming.

We still want our fiction writers to walk along the road with Balzac's mirror in hand reflecting back what's on every side, but we don't want them showing us merely the little of it that we've already seen. We want our writers to say what has been, until the moment we read it, known to us and yet unsayable. If it's a matter of preferring writers whose work speaks the truth about the known and as yet unsaid thing, I suppose that's aesthetics. But as Doris Lessing says, "Things change at the edges," and insofar as I myself want things to change, and I do, for this world as presently constituted is intolerable, then my ongoing affection for work written "on the edge" is political. I am still sufficiently optimistic to believe that if enough decent people see how bad things are on the borders, they will begin to change things there. And perhaps someday the center itself will be affected, however slightly. Perhaps someday it will not hold after all.

The stories and narratives (for some of them are in no conventional sense "stories") that I've selected here are in formal and stylistic terms wildly different from one another. They run the gamut from dead-on realism to hyper-text performance art, from strictly construed historical fiction to hermetic meditation. They are as long as seventeen pages and as short as one. White voices, black voices, male and female, with narrators speaking African-American English, Hispanic-American English, and Anglo-American English, talking high church and low, downtown and up-: these are the voices that daily surround us; and because they come to us, not from some dreamed-of center where no one in America lives anymore, but from the inescapable borderlands, they speak for us all.

A Confession

When Russell Banks and I agreed that our theme was to be *Borderlands*, we chose it partly for its open-endedness. Literally and figuratively, borderlands strike us as places where powerful forces come into contact with one another, where sparks fly. Specifically, it's the politics of that point of collision that we're interested in. Whatever else it does, all good art grapples with some tension, some conflict or argument, and our theme not only steered us straight into the fray, but also allowed for plenty of range. Theme, after all, does not define subject, or style, or attitude.

Before I began reading submissions for the issue, I decided to make some rough notes in order to articulate to myself exactly what it was I was looking for. Of the many poems that satisfied the thematic requirement, there would be far too many "good" ones to include. So how could I narrow my criteria in a way that would allow me to make a final selection based on some clear principle, some defined standard? What, in short, did I think were the most important qualities a poem should have?

I surprised myself when I made those notes, partly because it was easier than I'd anticipated to put into words my current critical beliefs/biases, and partly because I realized that they were much narrower, much sharper, than those I'd held only a few years ago. Poems that would have seduced me five years ago now didn't interest me much. Poems I'd have glanced at and passed over then now held my attention. I believe that because, if we are ambitious, we must evolve as writers, we must also evolve as readers. The poems in this issue are therefore a reflection of my own evolution as a writer and reader. A future fossil record, as it were, because I hope that five years from now that evolution will have continued, and what I'll want from poems will be something even clearer, more demanding.

Aesthetic distinctions always rest partly on personal under-structure. Let me admit that, and then dodge it. I don't wish to speculate here on matters of the self, but rather on the forms the self invents to understand and describe the essential nature of its interaction with the world and with art. It's not possible, though, to completely excise the presence of the personal, since it's clearly interlocked with any possible definition of critical taste. Therefore I want to give a sort of catalogue that describes the current state of my editorial soul, invoking the personal only when it seems unavoidable.

Five years ago, I believed that poems that were formally rough (I'd have said "sloppy") were unfinished poems. I wanted poems to have frictionless surfaces, or at least elegant, musically intentional frictions. Beauty in language, including purely decorative beauty, both musical and imagistic, seemed to almost justify itself, and could hold my attention. I wanted the poet to have been everywhere before me, cleaning and arranging, so that nothing seemed accidental or unconscious. Though I admired many poets whose work was generally acknowledged to be "political," the personal poem seemed to have more potential effectiveness and power than the overtly political one, which might verge on proselytizing, which made me uncomfortable. Lyric poems attracted me more than narrative ones, which seemed literal-minded and plodding most of the time, encumbered and shrunken by their stories. Structurally, a poem could successfully rest on a single delicate moment. Though I believed there was such a thing as truth and that poems should be truthful, I allowed for a lot of relativity. Truth appeared to exist on a sliding scale, depending on whose truth it was. In short, the perfect poem was a machine which could replicate the grief, beauty, and fascination of the individual poet's world, and contain it. It kept the tiger safely caged, so a reader could get close enough to smell it, be moved and even enlightened by it, without feeling the fear that is a kind of pain. Pain was okay, but I wanted it to be the pleasurable kind, the pang, the twinge, the clean surge of nostalgia, the moment of pure grief that's cathartic, the kind that passes quickly and leaves peace or exhilaration in its wake. Medicated pain.

The greatest grief of *my* life, at least so far, has been the death of nature as humankind has always known it. I was born in 1950, the year that TV first became widely available, the year in which the first of hundreds of new pesticides, herbicides, and preservatives burst into the food chain. Science was going to save the world from disease and drudgery. We'd won the Big War. There seemed to be no boundaries, not even space.

It's taken me the greater part of my adult life to confront the depth of my response to what has happened to the world—I mean nature, the world on which human life depends. I've done most of that work, emotional and intellectual, only in the last five years, though it's chafed at my consciousness since childhood. It's changed me, not the least as a writer and as a reader. It stripped away much of what I once admired or was entertained by in poems, incinerated it. It also burned away things that were obscuring poems I hadn't been able to appreciate before. It obliterated my patience for certain kinds of poems, and gave me new patience for other kinds.

Now, when I flip through a magazine or pull a book off the shelf in a bookstore, I'm still looking for poems that are bent on truth, but the hierarchies of that truth are far more sharply defined than they were, and much less malleable. Perhaps I'm simply old enough now to risk living outwardly with my convictions, no matter who might call me a fanatic, or worse. I believe that the planet—what we often call "the world"—is socially and ecologically threatened in a way that's unprecedented, and that most of us, expressly by being as conscious of it as we are, are in nearly total denial. I mean that most of us seem to feel anxiety about the hole in the ozone, the decimated rain forests, the carcinogens in our lives, etc., but we haven't really forced ourselves to fully imagine what it means beyond our immediate lives: whether or not there are syringes on the beach when we want to swim, whether we should take antioxidant supplements, or use a stronger sunscreen, or argue with the manager of the Grand Union about irradiated food. So I look for poems that aggress that denial, that fly under its radar, slip across its borders, plant bombs in its public buildings. I'm not talking about subject matter. The poems I love now do not have to be about pollution or our ever-more-hideous warfares (especially religious ones) or racism or sexism or the fact that we can put weapons in space but can't stop a man from putting his stepson in the trash compactor. But they do have to acknowledge consciousness of those things. They can't be innocent of death, or of what life is really like for most of the world's people, or the fact that our planet's condition as a patient is—in even the most optimistic opinion—guarded.

In terms of the task of editing, this means I now look hard at poems that carry the flags of outrage and grief, even if their surfaces are "rough." In fact, I've come to value highly some kinds of roughness because I believe they carry their cargos more honestly, in fact more precisely, by refusing to try to smooth unsmoothable edges. There are some things that cannot be said in purely beautiful language, places in a poem where we *ought* to stumble, or be brought up uncomfortably short, or hear an ugly sound. I'm fascinated by the lapses arrived at in this way, the residue of revisions resulting from honest mistakes, rude epiphanies, changes of heart, self-deceit when it's confronted and appropriated. Decoration—no matter how thrilling or gorgeous the image, how subtle, stirring, or elegant the music—now seems gratuitous and I have little patience with it. I call it prettification, and think it's nice in yards, parks, and department store windows. I trust the instincts of the unconscious, both the poet's and my own, more than I did. I no longer feel the need to apprehend a poem completely with each separate faculty; I'm more willing to float without panic in the space between intellect and emotion, for instance. I'm not very interested in poems that explore the personal without reference to the larger world. Such poems seem self-absorbed unless they're infected by death-consciousness. There was once a time when I'd tell people (without irony, alas) that I was an apolitical person. The best spin I can put on that now is that it was a sin of ignorance. All good poems are political poems—they *do* make something happen. The boundaries between kinds of poems seem less significant than they once did, whether a poem's a lyric, a meditation, a narrative. More interesting are impure fusions, hybrids that don't grow the way you expect. I still find the metaphor of poem-as-cage useful, but now see its point not as protecting the reader from the tiger, but in allowing him to get close enough to get clawed without getting killed. So my tolerance for poem-inflicted pain is higher than it used to be. In all of these ways, coming at something sidelong is often more frontal than coming at it head-on because the results are less predictable, more dangerous. Less controllable. More subversive of expectation. Thus, while clarity and straightforwardness of expression are still virtues, I do not so much value literalness, and this has of course changed my definition of precision. Recklessness is attractive, sometimes even crudeness, if it's used as a crowbar to pry the lid off something menacing. Less and less am I enamored of high polish, human experience presented in forms so technically sophisticated, musically and visually seductive, and "managed" that the wilderness is no longer visible. That's why even the metrical poems I've chosen here have their dukes up, and why I've included poems that some readers will think are too much in their face. It's hard to talk about these things in the abstract, but I don't have the space to give enough examples to show the range of what I mean. The poems in this issue are my examples.

So that's a confession of my current editorial bias. It's the invisible umbrella over all the poems you're about to read. Whether quiet or rowdy, they all have a clear and direct relation to the truth, which makes them passionate, precise, gutsy, and disturbing. In spite of their griefs, angers, and despairs, they're also full of the joy that comes from loving human life with abandon. I think of them as a friendly but anarchic crowd clamoring for change—good company in a dark age.

JAN RICHMAN

Origami for Adults

People who've seen relatives die by fire, stand
to the right of this line. People who've imagined large,
drug-taking siblings, crouch down by their feet and warm
your hands. People who offer syllogistic explanations
for plain brown acts, play musical minds to the tune
of any anthem. People who delay sobbing to answer
the telephone, people who voluntarily live in Nashville,
people who cheat by memorizing the eye chart at the DMV,
march down the main street of television wearing
your tongues on your sleeves. People who've said everything
necessary in one passionate round of naked defilement,
roam anywhere, like lucky ghosts, ingesting all of the whiteness
of lies, but none of the calories. People who do
what their fathers did, people who don't believe in death,
people who never think for a minute about stepping
out of your skins, join hands. We're going to play
Pass the Broom. People who want to be heroes, lie down
as flat as roads. People for whom a Presto log
is a harbinger of desire, people whose mouths have dried up
and healed over like blisters, people who've jumped
off bridges, ecstatic, only to be rescued by stubborn
fishermen, inhabit the chandeliers and drool down
on the rest of us with Christian pity. All together now:
Try not to conciliate. Try to stay inside
your own county lines.

Ajijic

The lengthy lawns of the rich run down
to the lake's lap. Cats steal *chiroles* from the nets
where they're drying on the shore. Dresses and jeans
lie flat below the fish, dancing an ancient, static line.
Their owners' hair floats in black, soapy masses
on the green sway. I'm stuck in jangling shade, no matter
where I walk, bored as a horse, flies in my vision.
The naked babies are held up, glistening brown.
At the lakeside café, Americans eat *seviche*
with tan, silvered hands. I came down to the water
to escape the feuding, infallible generations.
In my grandfather's eye is my father's eye, and so on.
There'll be green mango pie and tequila for supper.
The trucks will sing on the highway all night.
These clean girls will circle the plaza clockwise,
entwined in pairs, throbbing to be plucked from the wheel.
I'll dance in the bar with Mexican boys
who'll squeeze my ass and tell my white throat, You,
alone, are beautiful. The clothes pale as they dry,
the *chiroles* darken. A small girl throws sand
at the boldest cats and chatters, rolling her eyes.
They meet mine, then bolt away, as though
I could infect her with my gaze, unfasten her
from her familiar, exacting chore.
As though if I could, I would.

LAURA KASISCHKE

House Fable

There were always human handprints
on the walls, honey-

pawed in the kitchen, blood-red
in the bedroom: a house

built on snow, beaten
and teased and fed fish. The dog

dozed by the fire, breathed
orange dust from his nostrils and spit

out colored dirt. Behind the hearth
two children (the kidneys)

played with a pretty box; an old man (the head) slept
near them in a chair, and a young

married couple (the intestines) stood
kissing at the window. Out-

side, the valley was wandered with reindeer. Spring
came and the stairs

and orchid bulbs
ascended to nothing but sky. The clover

hid like hornets in the garden
beneath an enormous rock. *Grease*

flour feathers in the kitchen
and in the parlor the chiming of clocks. Some-

thing suckled, something starved. A sled
in the attic, and a waterfall

etched in an ashtray. *Send*
word soft-penciled in Russian

on the back of a postcard
of two old ladies in black standing

bent before a blurred gray fence: our
great-aunts Dominance

and Submission who died
at one another's hands.

Somewhere It Still Moves

I was having dinner with my friends Howie and Francine.
The restaurant was old, maybe five hundred years:
whitewashed walls, great black beams on the ceiling,
no windows. We felt we were in the midst of history.
As Americans, the past seemed absent from our country.
The waiter kept knocking his head with his fist, trying
to explain something. The only words we knew were Pivo-
beer and Dobro-good. Hitting his head like that,
we thought he was telling Howie he was stupid. First
he would form his hands into a circle, then he would give
his forehead a smack. The waiter wore a white jacket,
black pants. Perhaps he was twenty-five. Okay, said Howie,
sure. Bring it to me, whatever it is. This was Sarajevo,
the spring of 1989. A week of poetry readings, meeting
other poets, strolling with ice creams, attending the Saturday
night dance at the old hotel, no different than dances
I had attended in Iowa or Pennsylvania or Detroit.
Near the Princip Bridge a pair of bronze footprints
were set into the sidewalk. We each placed our feet
into these bronze souvenirs. This is where Princip stood
when he shot the Archduke and his wife. When the waiter
brought our dinner, there were our plates and on Howie's
plate a paper bag, like the bag in which a schoolboy
packs his lunch. Howie opened it carefully. Brains
in a bag, lamb brains cooked in a paper bag. We recalled
how the waiter made a circle, then knocked his forehead.
This was Howie's dinner. He was delighted. He could
barely breathe for all his laughter. We all laughed
and drank red wine. The other tables were filled
with happy people, men and women eagerly discussing
the subjects of their passions. When the door opened,
there was music from the streets and a warm breeze

smelling of foliage and the dust of a thousand years.
There was the constant clatter of silverware on dishes.
The waiter laughed with us. He is probably dead now.
Killed by a sniper as he crossed a street or stood
by a window. The restaurant, the entire block, has been
transformed into rubble, so many rocks at a crossroads.
I've seen pictures in the papers. And those other diners,
those easy eaters, those casual laughers? Some
on one side, some on the other, some blown to pieces,
some shot in the head. Scattered, scattered.
But all that came later. On one particular evening
the waiter brought his tray with a paper bag on a plate
and we laughed. A fragment of that sound is still traveling
so far out into the dark, an arrow perhaps glittering
in the flicker of distant stars. Somewhere it still moves.
I must believe that. Otherwise, nothing else in the world
is possible. We are the creatures that love and slaughter.

Santiago: Forestal Park

Teenagers and oldsters, married couples and lovers—
it is eight in the evening and everyone is kissing.
On park benches, on the grassy slopes of the hill,
sitting on curbs, joined in cafés they are kissing.

(I am not kissing; I am strolling along.
If I want activity, I have my newspaper.)

Why is the kissing so quiet? Thousands of lips
jostling together and not a whisper can be heard
above the buses rushing people home to recapture
the kissing they have missed.
                              If I could be anything,
I'd make myself into an orchestrator of kisses.
Instead of millions of kisses snapped off at random,
let them happen at once, a powerful smack
to rise above the roar of traffic, a smack to make
the generals glance up from their machinations.

Policemen, senators, dark-jowled funeral directors—
all jarred from narrow paths by the pedagogical kiss,
an explosion to hang like a pink cloud over the city.
It goes without saying people would change their lives.
I leave it to you to imagine how better we'd become.

My paper tells me the Year of the Monkey began yesterday;
a year of good fortune, a year bursting with happy babies.
I prowl through the park down a corridor of plane trees,
a gauntlet of benches and on each bench a couple kissing,
some are sprawling, fondling each other, heads on laps,
touching breasts, genitals, but always the silent kissing.

My solitude is like a big person walking by my side.
Some might say it is frightening, overbearing, cruel.
Nothing could be further from the truth. See how
kindly it takes my hand as we cross the busy street.

The Community

Had it worked well even once? Can one point
to a golden age of good times? Whatever
the case, the arms decided at last
to separate themselves. They were not

like the others; they had their own tastes
and ambitions: pleasures the others
could never appreciate. The legs went next,
alleging a life of agony within the community.

Hadn't they done the lion's share of work,
while forced to survive at the very bottom
of the human pile? Then the ribs went; the ears went.
The lungs extracted themselves and took the heart

because they needed a servant. The balls
appropriated the prick because they wanted
a bully. The eyes invited the nose
out of long friendship. Kidneys took the liver.

Leaving the tongue in the service of the lips,
the teeth marched off to their own village.
For a while everybody lived peacefully.
But then one heard that the hands had always

felt abused by the arms. And only the knees,
claimed the knees, knew what was good for knees.
If the feet felt downtrodden, then what about
the toes who left to form a community of ten?

And what about the toenails who without doubt
understood best what did best for toenails?
But after these further divisions, everybody
for a short time lived happily. Better not sing

if it meant being bossed by the tongue.
Better not feel, if it meant being beaten
by the heart. Better not lust, if it meant
being yanked up and downstairs by the prick.

But soon came additional discord—knuckles
could only be happy with other knuckles, hair
built its own hair ghetto, blood oozed in its own
private pool. Ponder the final drama of the teeth.

How could they have dreamt of life together?
Could the molars ever appreciate the true heart
of the incisors? Weren't the bicuspids destined
to live alone? And then the lower began to quarrel

with the upper, the left disparaged the right.
Stomach teeth, eye teeth, wisdom teeth, baby teeth!
Consider the two canines faced off on a dusty plain,
stamping and snarling and beating their chests.

Pastel Dresses

Like a dream, which when one
becomes conscious of it
becomes a confusion, so her name
slipped between the vacancies.

As little more than a child
I hurried among a phalanx
of rowdy boys across a dance floor—
such a clattering of black shoes.

Before us sat a row of girls
in pastel dresses waiting.
One sat to the right. I uttered
some clumsy grouping of sounds.

She glanced up to where I stood
and the brightness of her eyes
made small explosions within me.
That's all that's left.

I imagine music, an evening,
a complete story, but truly
there is only her smile and my response—
warm fingerprints crowding my chest.

A single look like an inch of canvas
cut from a painting: the shy complicity,
the expectation of pleasure, the eager
pushing forward into the mystery.

Maybe I was fourteen. Pressed
to the windows, night bloomed
in the alleyways and our futures
rushed off like shafts of light.

My hand against the small of a back,
the feel of a dress, that touch
of starched fabric, its damp warmth—
was that her or some other girl?

Scattered fragments, scattered faces—
the way a breeze at morning
disperses mist across a pond,
so the letters of her name

return to the alphabet. Her eyes,
were they gray? How can we not love
this world for what it gives us? How
can we not hate it for what it takes away?

Tenderly

It's not a fancy restaurant, nor is it
a dump and it's packed this Saturday night
when suddenly a man leaps onto his tabletop,
whips out his prick and begins sawing at it

with a butter knife. I can't stand it
anymore! he shouts. The waiters grab him
before he draws blood and hustle him
out the back. Soon the other diners return

to their fillets and slices of duck. How
peculiar, each, in some fashion, articulates.
Consider how the world implants a picture
in our brains. Maybe thirty people watched

this nut attack his member with a dull knife
and for each, forever after, the image pops up
a thousand times. I once saw the oddest thing—
how often does each announce this fact?

In the distant future, several at death's door
once more recollect this guy hacking at himself
and die shaking their heads. So they are linked
as a family is linked—through a single portrait.

The man's wobbly perch on the white tablecloth,
his open pants and strangled red chunk of flesh
become for each a symbol of having had precisely
enough, of slipping over the edge, of being whipped

about the chops by the finicky world, and of reacting
with a rash mutiny against the tyranny of desire.
As for the lunatic who was tossed out the back
and left to rethink his case among the trash cans,

who knows what happened to him? A short life,
most likely, additional humiliation and defeat.
But the thirty patrons wish him well. They all
have burdens to shoulder in this world and whenever

one feels the strap begin to slip, he or she thinks
of the nut dancing with his dick on the tabletop
and trudges on. At least life has spared me this,
they think. And one—a retired banker—represents

the rest when he hopes against hope that the lunatic
is parked on a topless foreign beach with a beauty
clasped in his loving arms, breathing heavily, Oh,
darling, touch me there, tenderly, one more time!

Can You Smell My Sandwich?

for John Casey

It is only ever about power, see. Pick the crowd and pick your vantage point, then watch. Learn the con, you have to learn to look for what does not originate in ordinary. Hats will tow you in; and shoes. One good hour on watched shoes you learn the lessons of lost civilizations. Hats and bald men, true, the classic duo, followed only by plain women and red fingernails, women who've been told their hands are pretty, or their hands are soft, or their hands are like those hands that handle anything and everything expressively from toilet rolls to dog food on TV for money. Don't let yourself ignore the shoes. Don't discount feet, in general. In men you want to look for loafers, and you want to educate your eye for size. Disregard the loafered foot beyond size twelve, it is not the well-heeled secret. People, even men, of big feet do not cultivate a secret vanity about their pediments, men with small feet nearly always do. Men with small feet have been told for years they have "nice" feet by shoe clerks and by women, guaranteed, and they've allowed this praise, innocuous as rice, to lodge somewhere in the tooth that butts the tooth that makes the inward grin of what we call Conceit, the pearly grit of our existence, cleansed by ego, licked by love, the untaxed vice, the syntax of the self expressing self, *the secret vanity,* and we each and every one of us has at least a single one, a pair of pretty hands, small feet, small wrists, some aspect of our forehead not dissimilar to Garbo's or to Einstein's, name it. Name it, please. Find it and you own that person. Spot it and you're in. It's voodoorama time and I'm so good at it they ought to elevate me onto postage, paste my face on stamps, food stamps. I'm onto something here with this lady on the seat in front of me, eyeing her for stops, when what should happen but old trouble hauls his ass on like unbonded freight, sees me, spots the con, and takes a crucial place not letting on he's interrupting. Diz. The doodah man. The mentholated small craft warning. Voodoo wizard. What the hell you doing on my bus I let him know by looking, but the law of shared existence mediates between us. One man's bus is still another one's performance space, so hey. Streets, you either love them or you hate them, like the theater; like church. Meanwhile this lady's twisting in her seat as Diz skids in, trying to inhale the flesh of her own nose, sucking in her nostrils in that can-you-smell-my-sandwich kind of way. "People and they's food," I throw to Diz. "See you clocking and they think you after they's brown bag."

"Zatso," Diz muses.

"Court disaster to protect they's food."

"Oh mmmmmmm?"

"They's Walkmen."

"Mmm?"

"They's babies."

Diz teaches you that you need to learn to love what feeds you, lick the streets or they lick you. Diz has been a Village indigent since Nixon, has a union card, and he can state his numbers, veteran's, tax, probation, zip, phone, date of discharge, dosage, sun's diameter. I think he said once he was from Kentucky, but he allows you to believe he's from the state you're from. Sure I know where that is, he can say about a hometown, any hometown, I'd always wisht I'd been from there, in case your vanity is place. "California Girl" will still rekindle glimmers in a certain kind of woman, and Eurotrash still pay for Euro-fawning, but vanity as place is not the vanity it used to be upon these shores. *What do I ask?* Diz stakes. Spare change. What do I give? A fair exchange. Not every person on the streets is a philosopher. The System, Diz explains, is just another cardboard box. The gates of heaven are two heating grates, a city thanks its dwellers with a gift of ample gratefulness. Baths, a dime. Baths, two bits with towel. Baths, two dollars, own your soap. When did beggars turn into "The Homeless," when did everybody ever have a home, you take a nation by the neck and shake it you can hear its secret vanity inside. Prosperity—where the hell did all these poor come from, send in the Marines, send flares up, son, the sky is falling, folks are landing in your yards. Let the dogs loose, boy, and call for backup. All we have to do is look into your secret vanity, as through a windowpane and, Flynn, guess what, we're in. The poor of any nation own no vanity. The poor of any nation are not vain. A duck can beg. A chicken in the yard comes out begging, chicken with a brain not even half the size of its own gizzards, monkeys beg, and cats and dogs and carp in ponds, but only humans beg from their own species, only humans trade their labor, openly, for food. Or trade a smile for change. Or trade a word for bread. Or trade a promise, or a trick. A city does not shelter like an ancient keep, sleep takes the form of prison, you can die in it. If only we was wolves, Diz says. I'd marry you, that simple. I'd rather we was fish, I state. Big fish? Diz baits. Full and high and silvery, I paint. Diz messes in my drift. Did you say "high"? he feints. His hands are large, his hands are huge, and Baby Hands was what he called me when I started hanging on his corner. He watched to see if that could put a blush on me but he was wrong, because it couldn't. I'm not vain about my hands. My hands are small but I'm not vain about them. I'm not vain about my feet and they are smallish, too, he could have called me Baby Feet or Baby Shoes, if I had shoes. I'm not vain about my hair, if I have hair, and I'm not vain about my looks if I have any. I'm not vain about my children rest their souls and I'm not vain about accomplishments. I'm not vain about this way I dress. I'm not vain for graduating high school or for running track. I'm not vain for kissing Mikey Dorwart in the seventh grade. I'm not vain for hardscrabble and scramble egg the special way I fry or vain about the kitchen things I could remember if I wanted to or vain about my pussy vain about the fact I never cry and won a prize in English named for William Faulkner worth ten dollars cash. I'm not vain about the things that I once knew about the mystery of perseverance, why heat rises and hopes fall. Walk out on a man one day and soon somebody calls out pretty lady, pretty darling, strut that stuff this way, no references; a scrap. Even if you don't drink everyone you meet is either crazy with religion or a drug, or righteous with possession of a certified philosophy about the virtue of hard work. Even if you have your health your looks will go, can't make it in the rural what you have a car and someone tells you jobs are waiting in the population centers, and the point about the point from which you always start is that you'd never do it if you knew how you are gonna end. You think, This is only temporary. This is just a setback. I'll wait here until I'm warmer. Even if you keep your shoes your legs will blister. People's lives go downhill for as many reasons as there are to count and you can count on no one, Diz will tell you, which I'd like to think is not the whole unholy truth. The streets aren't any place for women, you ought to get into a shelter, Baby Hands, go back to your Southern heaven, Diz directs.

"Diz," I hiss. "Your inconvenient self is sitting between me and dinner."

"Can't be helped," he says. "I'm flirtin'."

"Not with me, I'm fixed."

"Every person who is broke believe she fixed," he taunts.

People acting like you're not exactly sleeping in their walking space. People making detours all around you. People looking scared and challenged by your empties. This is where I live, my memory my walls, my bones my stairs, my stares my windows my façade. This is me upon my picket fence the mortgage paid the lawn well waged, the wickets, gravel and magnolia, rice and beans a chicken in the pot a light on in the window, cedar shake and cedar shingle, asphalt siding, roto-rooter, weedkill, accident and casualty, a priest will come to bless this house a house is not a home a home is where the heart is, home is where your vanity is hidden. I look at Diz's hands. The lady in the seat in front of us is gathering her bags, twisting to avoid the sight of us, her back a statement of her rigid purpose. And Diz's hands are fucking huge, those pitchblack frostbit fingertips, a broken tooth, a face increased by weather, hard to say why some stay as they are, but that's the nature of a monument, it never moves. That's the nature of a fairy tale, it never changes.

The lady stands and I stand, too, which makes her look at me, a trick Diz taught me, make them think you're going to follow them and they will turn toward you unconsciously an instant to assess the threat and right when she is staring at me I sit down again and smile and lean toward her, the seat between us, "Couldn't help but hearing you were humming," I stage-whisper and I shake my head a little, like a gourd in a mariachi band, never letting her release her gaze, I lean in closer, hesitate, and then I say, "I bet you used to be the best one in the choir.... Don't you, Diz?"

"Without a doubt," the doodah man recounts.

I wish you could have seen what comes into her eyes.

She starts with five and ends with twenty.

Someone once, when she was young, had said her voice could bring down Heaven.

"I always fancied I could sing," she's saying, fussing with the wallet.

Here, take this.

And take this, too.

It's the sandwich I was going to have for lunch.

You'll like it.

It's brisket.

Two stops later Diz says, "Baby, are we getting off?"

But someone else is getting on and I say, Diz, you doodah man. Hand me that glass slipper.

The Baby on the Table

Everything is so dark under the baby, the table
floats legless,
    a rectangle of light. Around it
the angels are bending their doctoral faces,
    the baby unswaddled,
undisturbed.
    But can you see them? See the kleigs
bearing down on the infant, throwing up a stark light
    on the angels' faces, how Mary
seeps into the black floor, dress vanishing
    in its deepening
folds?
    She is a head, a moon, floating without expression
above her naked child,
    the distance between them filling with ready,
angels bending closer in a luminous cone—
    Will they do it? Will they dip their hands
into the light?
    Will they fish out its heart, its lungs, its soul
like an aspirin, lifting it bloodless
    from the milky white?
Must there come a time, a line, a moment, a stanza
    where I say

On February 9th, 1965, I was slit through the belly
    without anesthetic
to remove a gangrenous illium? To make you look
    in the sterile bucket at the side
of the gurney,
    at the blackened, pussed, and stinking intestine,
to tap your shoulder and look in your face asking
    Is that you? Is that you?
Have you ever been hurt, have you ever been cut, is it only

physical knives?
Is this how I write about
   the baby on the table? By looking at a
poor black-and-white print of a nameless Adoration
   by the school of Jan-Stephan Von Calcar?
The print is so poor, is that an egg, a star
   through the trees in the distance,
are they sheep, are they men,
   kneeling under its light? I can't tell
if they are bending in lamentation or praising
   hallelujah, if the egg
is a cross
   in a circle of light—when will they lower

the kiss, the fist, the sharpened
   scalpel, the angels
are waiting, calm, impassive, the emanations
   of science
in each white face—
   Can you help me sew up
what they're about to open? Can you feel
   the chill of the table
on your own small back?
   I keep looking at the baby again and again,
outlined on the table by a membrane
   of shadow,
how it looks up at the sky unconcerned— Where
   is the fault
in this studied composure? Where is the crack in the gloss
   over suffering,
is it here, at the base, where the paint is chipping,
   revealing the starkness beneath? Look in there,
in the fissures between
   the blackened oils, and see the form
of your very own cross,
   slipping through the vent in the hospital nursery
and alighting on your chest your chosen
   star,
marking you for the scalpels of light.

Hardie

You know how tiny kids walk up to you, raise their arms
and expect to be picked up—I used to do that; that was me.

Me, with my diaper full and my nose half-crusty.

I remember being eye to eye with the little doors
underneath the kitchen sink—I was a child seriously.

I used to yank open those cabinets and see the shiny colors
and glass: the orange box of Tide, the pink bottle leaking
dishwashing liquid, a green Pine Sol thing with big yellow letters.

Of course, I couldn't read and before I could touch anything
my mom was snatching me back, slapping my hands—

that shit hurt! My hands were really little, really
new, like shoots fresh out of the ground,
really soft—I was a child. Is that clear?

People just put me to bed whenever they felt like it.
People sat me on the potty every other whenever
and said *Go!*

I didn't have any words, just sloppy, muddy kinds of garbled
    clucks
that wanted to be words, that tried to be wordish—

Think of the amount of criticism I got. Criticism piled on
like cold cream of wheat.

It was like I couldn't do anything right—not a goddamn thing!

Picture *me* in a high chair being pressured to eat—
they might have been dangling a secret agent off a cliff
trying to make him give up something top-secret—

I was little; my legs hardly held me up; everybody
stood around poised to catch me—
Ooops! Oooopsy! Whoops-a-daisy!

How could I get my confidence?

But now I'm big, I eat ice cream all the time—I'm big; I use
the *Men's* room; nobody tells me what to do,

even though I feel like I'm holding on to my life the way a
wounded ant clings to a window screen. I'm

big now. Big and musty. Big enough to hide my baby shoes
in the palm of one hand.

But once I was a kid. I didn't
need deodorants. I sat on my grandmother's lap
and ate candy spearmint leaves.

I wasn't down on white people. I
didn't even know I was black. My whole bag
was cartoons—I was a child, goddammit!

Just a mouthful of Tonka Toys and Lego,
a little guy with no sense of time passing.
Where was everybody going? What happened to *Johnny Quest*?!

Next thing I know, I got this *hardie* thumping around on my
    belly—
every morning, fearless, like my own bad-ass rooster—
sun-up and *cock-a-doodle-doo*! I couldn't pee with it and
nobody would tell me what it was for.

I wasn't always so worldly. I wasn't always a madman
over women's legs, either. I spent my first fifteen years
without a real kiss.

I was a child. You think I don't remember?!
You think it's easy keeping all this innocence pent up inside?!

And now, when it comes to money, I'm like some dizzy insect
full of wanting it, like some big bluebottle fly
tipsy over a mound of shit.

I wasn't always like this.

Parts of me starting getting large, growing hair:
my underarms, my wrists, even the tops of my feet.

But I *was* a little boy once: really curious, really small, really
    scared—

Is that clear?

On the Ambiguity of Injury and Pain

When I saw the x-ray of my boy's broken bones
the young doctor held up to the light
a fist closed around my heart.
Behind us in the gurney he was lost
in his pain, betrayed by the world
like birds by false spring.
The little Mozart piece
would be abandoned
to summer evenings
jangled out of time.
And back at school his classmates
rush to him in wonder at his wound
and scratch their names into the plaster.
And tonight when I bathe him he is shy.
When I try to run the soap
and rag between his legs
he stops me with his free hand
the way I've been stopped by women.
We move in the old way around each other.
Kisses so sweet. Dark room of joy.

Bear Meadow

In this field of day lilies
just opening, beating for sun
in this lush summer bear meadow,
I tried to find a way
to stay in your world, wife.
The field hummed with life,
the bugs and frogs
and jeering birds
but no words came
as I had hoped
from the sky
blue as a marble.
I tried to lose myself
in the woods of beyond
but only paths fell under my feet
and I glimpsed the shape
that nature is
unfolding in the roots
and limbs connecting us
with threads of light
but then so quickly gone.
I could imagine
an emptiness without you,
without your face
in my hands
like a flower
I could imagine something
bottomless and cold.
We have traveled
deep into the center
of something we can't name
yet stayed side by side
when the light died
and the road ground down

to a cutbank through trees
and there was nowhere to run.
What I have to give you
I feel in my blood
like many small fires
burning into one.

The Borders

To say that she came into me,
from another world, is not true.
Nothing comes into the universe
and nothing leaves it.
My mother—I mean my daughter did not
enter me. She began to exist
inside me—she appeared within me.
And my mother did not enter me.
When she lay down, to pray, on me,
she was always ferociously courteous,
fastidious with Puritan fastidiousness,
but the barrier of my skin failed, the barrier of my
body fell, the barrier of my spirit.
She aroused and magnetized my skin, I wanted
ardently to please her, I would say to her
what she wanted to hear, as if I were hers.
I served her willingly, and then
became very much like her, fiercely
out for myself.
When my daughter was in me, I felt I had
a soul in me. But it was born with her.
But when she cried, one night, such pure crying,
I said I will take care of you, I will
put you first. I will not ever
have a daughter the way she had me,
I will not ever swim in you
the way my mother swam in me and I
felt myself swum in. I will never know anyone
again the way I knew my mother,
the gates of the human fallen.

1954

Then dirt scared me, because of the dirt
he had put on her face. And her training bra
scared me—the newspapers, morning and evening,
kept saying it, *training bra,*
as if the cups of it had been calling
the breasts up—he buried her in it,
perhaps he had never bothered to take it
off. They found her underpants
in a garbage can. And I feared the word
eczema, like my acne and like
the X in the paper which marked her body,
as if he had killed her for not being flawless.
I feared his name, Burton Abbott,
the first name that was a last name,
as if he were not someone specific.
It was nothing one could learn from his face.
His face was dull and ordinary,
it took away what I'd thought I could count on
about evil. He looked thin and lonely,
it was horrifying, he looked almost humble.
I felt awe that dirt was so impersonal,
and pity for the training bra,
pity and terror of eczema.
And I could not sit on my mother's electric
blanket anymore, I began to have a
fear of electricity—
the good people, the parents, were going to
fry him to death. This was what
his parents had been telling us:
Burton Abbott, Burton Abbott,
death to the person, death to the home planet.

The worst thing was to think of her,
of what it had been to be her, alive,
to be walked, alive, into that cabin,
to look into those eyes, and see the human.

for Stephanie Bryan

Six Pieces

The Low Road

Soon she headed into the wind. Sepulveda Boulevard would lead her to the cornfields and crows of Scripture, a field gullied by rainfall, and parking lots where men sat in cars smoking. Sometimes they got out of their cars and went to the bathroom in a cement barrack. This action scared her back to creation. Rows of electric lights burned white in the daylight under a plastic tent. A model airplane buzzed across the field, but she was forbidden entrance to that nature preserve because she walked with a dog. Encircled by mountains, the valley was a catcher for fog. Early mist dreamed over the dam. Brittle twigs screened her view. Berries bled blue but were gray with dew, too. Two bodies had lain in mud the night before as she bolted across the San Diego Freeway. Yellow canvas covered them and she flinched to avoid a blue raindrop heading for her eye. Police lights were on the way. She had noticed earlier that angels, like mourning doves, coo to a Pyrrhic meter. Later she would take the bread-soaked square in wine from an Eastern Orthodox priest and pray for these bodies. But that night she continues on past the end of their lives to the recycling center with her daily bag of cans.

Everything's a Fake

Caiote scruff in canyons off Mulholland Drive. Fragrance of sage and rosemary, now it's spring. At night the mockingbirds ring their warnings of cats coming across the neighborhoods. Like castanets in the palms of a dancer, the palm trees clack. The HOLLYWOOD sign has a white skin of fog across it where erotic canyons hump, moisten, slide, dry up, swell, and shift. They appear impatient—to make such powerful contact with pleasure that they will toss back the entire cover of earth. She walks for days around brown trails, threading sometimes under the low branches of bay and acacia. Bitter flowers will catch her eye: pink and thin honeysuckle, or mock orange. They coat the branches like lace in the back of a mystical store. Other deviant men and women live at the base of these canyons, closer to the city, however. Her mouth is often dry, her chest tight, but she is filled to the brim with excess idolatry. It was like a flat mouse—the whole of Los Angeles she could hold in the circle formed by her thumb and forefinger. Tires were planted to stop the flow of mud at her feet. But she could see all the way to Long Beach through a tunnel made in her fist. Her quest for the perfect place was only a symptom of the same infection that was out there, a mild one, but a symptom nonetheless.

There Are No "Others"

Outside the plant they walked hurriedly, she a few paces behind him, her voice raw and loud. Her right hand held tight to the swinging bed for baby, invisible in a mashed potato-ish heap of cottons and quilts. The man was dressed entirely in black, wore a tight black net on his hair, sweated lightly through his dewy black skin. Her bleached yellow hair expressed no cowardice, but rage, so they both (because together) suffered all the way from the plant to the car. "What kind of girl is this—an empty shell? a lonely cell in which an empty soul must dwell?" Colors are identified with the state of the spirit. The Regency Arms, for example, were red in welcoming her every night, both as anarchist arms and as sexual arms. Red lips on a tropical neon sign read REAL LIVE NUDES. Mini-malls held gourmet shops along Sunset Boulevard. Her talk all the way to the click of the car door was really a scream. Why was he taking it so passively? others wondered watching. But in such a case there are no answers adequate outside of "jailbait." Dogs piss on a rhododendron bush, meantime, hit a small piece of script reading JESUS COSMOS. It was the Sabbath when all things begin anew, and all things are considered equal, and when, as in dreams, the new and the equal know no evil.

Jailbait

A trough inside the Pacific Ocean led to an onshore flow. Then high seas, large swells, and a small-craft advisory. One storm system was weaker than the one before, and so did nothing to shift around the ozone, carbon monoxide, nitrogen dioxide, or the pre-menstrual syndrome in women's bodies. From the South-land mountains into the valley, clouds pumped out shadows and rainbows. Palm leaves played on invisible keys, and the only children on the streets of Hollywood were lost children. Just as jazz makes white wine chill on a balcony, so black stockings make syringes look like silver, and nostril rings resemble Disney tattoos. Shelter couches have rough skins and are not welcoming. Leather gloves, rip-hemmed jeans, sneakers, and Benadryl, all for sale. Kiss my casket, said one of nine thousand inmates. Two thousand have been given antibiotics against an outbreak of meningitis. One individual lay on a mattress in an unlighted cell, listening. It had to be a detour he was experiencing. He had hoped for notoriety when the means of his survival were found in obscurity. When he had begun performing actions that he knew were expected of him, he had already begun to lose his way. Now protected by darkness that his interior met with lighted, colorized dream stories, he could live without gas or refrigeration. He had come to this condition without even making a choice. It was rather as if someone had stuck up a sign on the lonely highway, and he had obeyed it, although it turned out to have been a joke intended for someone else to laugh about.

You Can't Warm Your Hands in Front of a Book
But You Can Warm Your Hopes There

Feathers fluffed the ashtray bin at the bottom of the elevator. Feathers and a smeared black look littered the parking lot like mascara. A cage would glide back and let them out to merge with the other cars on La Brea. It looked as if a struggle had ended in tears between the bird and an enemy. She broke through the fear to examine it. No chicken claws, or comb, no wing, no egg. The neutrality of words like "nothing" and "silence" vibrated at her back like plastic drapes. How could there be a word for silence? A child's lips might blow, the North wind bring snow, a few stars explode, boats rock, but whatever moved in air did not by necessity move in ears and require the word "silence" therefore. She had personally sunk to a level where she could produce thought, and only "violence" remained a problem. It was common in her circle. A bush could turn into a fire, or a face at a clap of the hand could release spit and infection. The deviants were like herself unable to control their feelings. Los Angeles for them was only hostile as a real situation during the rainy season when torrents ripped down the sides of the canyons and overnight turned them sloshy. Then they hid in underground places, carrying Must the Morgue Be My Only Shelter?? signs. But the rest of the time the sort of whiteness spread out by a Southland sun kept them warm, and they could shit whenever they wanted to, in those places they had long ago staked out. My personal angel is my maid, said one to another, putting down his Rilke with a gentle smile.

My Song, My Only Song Goes:
One Is My Lucky Number!

Her sneakers were wearing down to two gnarled scoops, but she was never surprised that the vertical pronoun was also a number. On the apophatic path you choose to stay at the edge of the central city where you get a quasi-this and a quasi-that. In the diplomatic world transparency means non-ideological, neutral. In the walking world, it means eternal, invisible. One day clouds muffin against a tinny sky. L.A.'s a dirt heap, really, stuck with green nettles. A better shape to live in than the slabbish city. Cold and square as Forest Lawn. Why put a cake on a plate before putting it in your mouth? Why use a napkin instead of a sleeve to wipe away the dribble? I mean when I was walking the streets...she couldn't conceive of her own loneliness. Captain bass-playing melodies got to it, though, a black sax, like a foot-bridge over cognac. New York is a whole deal. Yoni, scared as a red anarchist, was given to every woman. Even her stepsister could say it twice. And her stepsister would say, exactly the way she would, "My stepsister hoped I would fail." B-minus was her score. She began by a drink or three to keep her moving down lubricated avenues. There the faces of brown-skinned boys presented her with the problem of beauty. Africa refused to leave them alone in America. For this great act of mercy she was happy: for them there would be no erasure! Their beauty was a promise that couldn't be broken, it was Adam getting Even, it was as basic as a billy club. Let the academics sneer at the Jesuits, and go on being the hypocritical clerics of the century, she at least dared to believe in retribution. While one derelict liked malt, barley, and high altitudes, most of the others like herself preferred a cloud of mimosa breaking down the chicken wire, and feet firmly planted on the names of the stars embossed in Hollywood Boulevard. She had her private "names for the days of the weak"—Man Day, Dues Day, Wine Day, Thirst Day, Fried Day, Sat-Around Day, and God's Day. These were written in the ground under her body's weight, where she was pleased to keep them.

The Curtain

Just over the horizon a great machine of death is roaring and
    rearing.
One can hear it always. Earthquake, starvation, the ever-
    renewing field of corpse-flesh.
In this valley the snow falls silently all day and out our window
We see the curtain of it shifting and folding, hiding us away in
    our little house,
We see earth smoothened and beautified, made like a fantasy, the
    snow-clad trees
So graceful in a dream of peace. In our new bed, which is big
    enough to seem like the north pasture almost
With our two cats, Cooker and Smudgins, lying undisturbed in
    the southeastern and southwestern corners,
We lie loving and warm, looking out from time to time.
    "Snowbound," we say. We speak of the poet
Who lived with his young housekeeper long ago in the
    mountains of the western province, the kingdom
Of complete cruelty, where heads fell like wilted flowers and
    snow fell for many months across the mouth
Of the pass and drifted deep in the vale. In our kitchen the
    maple-fire murmurs
In our stove. We eat cheese and new-made bread and jumbo
    Spanish olives
That have been steeped in our special brine of jalapeños and
    garlic and dill and thyme.
We have a nip or two from the small inexpensive cognac that
    makes us smile and sigh.
For a while we close the immense index of images
    which is
Our lives—for instance, the child on the Mescalero reservation
    in New Mexico in 1966

Sitting naked in the dirt outside his family's hut of tin and
    cardboard,
Covered with sores, unable to speak. But of course the child is
    here with us now,
We cannot close the index. How will we survive? We don't and
    cannot know.
Beyond the horizon a great unceasing noise is undeniable. The
    machine
May break through and come lurching into our valley at any
    moment, at any moment.
Cheers, baby. Here's to us. See how the curtain of snow wavers
    and falls back.

February Morning

The old man takes a nap
too soon in the morning.
His coffee cup grows cold.

Outside the snow falls fast.
He'll not go out today.
Others must clear the way

to the car and the shed.
Open upon his lap
lie the poems of Mr. Frost.

Somehow his eyes get lost
in the words and the snow,
somehow they go

backward against the words,
upward among the flakes
to the blankness of air,

the busy abundance there.
Should he take warning?
Mr. Frost went off, they say,

in bitterness and despair.
The old man stirs and wakes,
hearing the hungry birds,

nuthatch, sparrow, and jay
that clamor outside, unfed,
and words stir from his past

like this irritable sorrow
of jay, nuthatch, and sparrow,
wrath which no longer takes

shape of sentence or song.
He climbs the stairs to bed.
The snow falls all day long.

LAURIE SHECK

Rain

I can hear the rain now, its vanishing
averted glance, and long branches
descending softly toward cool water.
And then a voice coming back from its solitude
to find me, "When nothing spoke to me anymore
the broken statues spoke to me," and
"Be opened my mouth, untie what is upon my mouth."

I have betrayed a stillness.
I remember the statue's immaculate face,
the smooth white marble of her eyes.
And her hair so narrowly plaited
like a stringent hunger for order,
her hair like closure, the denial of regret.
How cold she was, how meticulously stranded.

Are those footsteps on the stairs now?—
a click, a jangled lock,
the rasp of cloth rubbing up against a doorway,
a rustling of sacks dropped down on a counter.
It must be my neighbor returning home from work,
and that noise—what is it now?—the drone
of a documentary he's turned on, its soundtrack

threading through the burned and looted
village, the mother and her starving child.
The music from the soundtrack touches down
onto the child's skin, filters briefly down,
a momentary softness, though by now, as the film
is played, replayed, the child must be dead,
dry earth blindly over it.

The rain has stopped, though it still rushes
in a downward motion from the trees
when the wind comes up in gusts.
My neighbor is quiet—maybe he is sleeping
or watching how the streetlamps
burn like a slow acid through the branches.
I can hear the sound of the sea, though it's far off,
as if it's moved into these trees nearby us
where over and over it shatters itself to be made whole.

The Afterlife

Then came the day even as the water glass felt heavy
and I knew, as I'd suspected, I grew lighter.
I grew lighter, yes.
Say, have you ever fainted?
Such a distinct horizon as you are raised above
your pain, like Chekhov's, *and it was clear to them the end*
was still far off . . .
or, *after forty years they entered Canaan . . .*
Don't tell me about turning from what might change you,
taking the second, not the first compartment
in the revolving door,
tossing the note in the bottle back into the channel.
No, the afternoon was not a practice for another.
The birds, they flew.
The virus spread through the city.
It was a real day, and I grew lighter.
And I asked my friend if I could hold his arm
to keep myself from rising.
I picked up rare city stones and put them in my pocket.
Still, I could see how the buildings dreamed themselves
backwards to rubble, and the sun-smashed
windows, the mortar back to sand.
I watched Orpheus in the flesh set broken china
into the fissures of the sidewalk after he'd poured the grout
and smoothed it with his trowel.
Then, blue shard by blue shard he made a sky of the abyssal
sepulchers across which the homeless
floated, much as I, where
the trains passed, and the ground shook.
It was like standing inside singing, knowing something of its
  need.
It was the troubled child grown old, happy, the lost in sight

of home, and born for this.
There is a sadness older than its texts
that will outlive the language,
like the lover who takes you by the roots of your hair.
In this way I was awake, I was light,
I grew lighter,
though I had not yet been lifted.

The Story

Innocent and earnest, good at marathons, the surgeon
believed in his hands; he said
he'd cut the tumor out, a convoluted unnatural thing
wrapping its tentacles around the brain's little house.
Nothing more than architecture, then he paused:
he knew about the maze, the puzzle.
He put on his white clothes; over his entire being
he laid white cloth, he gathered his men
and the one woman, and they all went in
with sharp instruments. The drill took the bone
and the red spray flew. They found the right room
in the back of the head. They found the tiny monster heart
wavering near the brain stem.

But no microscope could turn down the folds
of the pineal gland, where the soul looked out
its infinite window and saw the altered light.
Saw the giant hand that was not God's.
No scalding oil fell, the soul did not shiver
and hide its face. The light of science
went on burning, and so did the knife,
dismantling cell by cell. But the soul was calm.
It waited out the industrious nine-hour sleep,
dozing itself at times to avoid the blinding
overhead lamp. The soul sang its little songs,
dreamless infant songs: far beneath and years gone,
complimentary to the Mozart the surgeon played.
Humming away, the soul wove a tuneless cover
for every memory of intrusion, fear, and pain.

And when you woke—
cut even where the clamps had held the mask to your face,
bandaged and swollen and clean,
changed but for the wide pacific blue of your eyes—
love still lay there: handsome, without innocence,
and utterly faithful.

LEON ROOKE

The Boy from Moogradi and the Woman with the Map to Kolooltopec

for Melissa and Ricardo
of Melissa's Piano Bar
Santorini, Greece

A re they crazy?"
"Yes."

"I think my officers would like to shoot these crazy people."

"Of course. But their deaths would reflect badly upon me."

A white woman and two white male companions lay unmoving on the ground, on their bellies, their hands tied behind their heads. They lay in swirling pools of mud and water, rivulets coursing about them and gushing down the mountainside. A handful of soldiers, dressed in rags, dark-skinned and solemn, armed with knives and rifles, stood guard over them, displaying only marginal interest.

"If my officers shoot you as well then your honor would be salvaged."

The speaker had given his name as Raoul; he was questioning a boy of about twelve, who had not yet been asked how he was called.

A heavy, warm rain was falling, with great monotony, as had been the case for the past several weeks.

"Tell the crazy people if they move my officers will shoot them."

"They will not move."

The man poked the woman with his rifle, lifting her hair so that he could see her burnished neck. He stood between her spread legs, his shoulders slumped under the drenching rain. Around them there existed a gnarl of twisty vines and trees, and leafy, swollen vegetation, and mountains rising another ten thousand feet, though they could not see beyond their own weary group because of the rain's steady downpour.

"What is the journey of these crazy people?"

"Their mission is to find Kolooltopec."

"But Kolooltopec does not exist."

"I agree."

"It does not matter whether you agree. I could agree also, but this would not change the matter."

"Yes," the boy said. "Because Kolooltopec still would not exist and you and I would both be as crazy as these gringos."

"Yes."

"Good. Then we are in agreement."

The man stepped from between the woman's legs and stretched his naked arm around the boy's shoulder. They remained that way for some minutes, the three on the ground silent and unmoving, their faces all but buried within the coursing water, and the swarthy officers with their rifles muttering to themselves as they watched the rain and each other and their bedraggled prisoners on the ground.

"How long have you been on this journey with the crazy people?"

"Five days."

"Along the river?"

"Two days along the river. Then we began our ascent of the mountains."

"In the rain?"

"Yes."

"Then you must be from Ooldooroo. Or Moogradi."

"Moogradi. It is the village of my people."

"Does Ooldooroo still exist? We have heard rumors."

"I do not know."

The man fell silent for a moment, as a few of the men nearby spoke nervously of the apparent destruction of Ooldooroo.

"One of my officers came from Moogradi. He spoke well of the river basin and its people."

The boy nodded.

"He is dead three years now, this man from Moogradi."

The boy made a quick, violent sign of the cross, and each of the several officers within hearing did likewise, with murmurs of pain and astonishment that lifted above the rain. One of the prisoners coughed and made to stretch his legs, but quit this when he was nudged by one of the officers' rifles.

"It is a poor place, Moogradi."

"Yes."

"An affliction. Do you agree?"

"Yes."

"Nothing stinks so much as Moogradi."

"Yes."

"The men of Moogradi do nothing all day long, while the women work. Is this true?"

"Yes."

The man laughed.

"But the women are all ugly in Moogradi, especially the young girls. That is what I have heard."

"It is very true," the boy said. "But bless them anyhow."

The man laughed harder and pounded his hand merrily on the boy's shoulder. All the officers were laughing now and passing lewd comments back and forth.

"Whereas, Ooldooroo."

All fell silent.

The three on the ground lay as though stricken and the warm rain continued to fall and the rivulets to course noisily down the mountainside.

"What is your name, boy from Moogradi?"

"Toodoo."

"Is Toodoo a good name?"

"It is my parents' good name."

"But you have ugly sisters."

"Yes."

All laughed again, including the boy, although his face was strained and he looked on the point of exhaustion. He did not believe this man standing beside him, with a hand on his shoulder, was the famous desperado Raoul.

"My dead officer from Moogradi was a Frooloo. Do you know the Frooloo family of Moogradi?"

The boy looked out into the rain. The entire Frooloo family, a long time ago, had disappeared; if the officer asking him so many questions was the famous desperado Raoul, he would know this.

The man took his hand from the boy's shoulder and once again stood between the woman's split legs. He regarded the woman's backside solemnly for a while, before kneeling and doing something with the ropes binding her hands. Rainwater coursed down his face, which was without expression.

"No? Then perhaps my dead officer lied. Perhaps he had never seen Moogradi. Or perhaps the Frooloos of Moogradi are also in journey towards Kolooltopec."

The man smiled. The boy tried to smile back, but he was too tired.

The woman lifted her shoulders somewhat and covered her face with her hands. Then she slumped down again and lay motionless.

A number of the officers slung their rifles and threaded their way carefully through the underbrush and sat down out of the rain, under a rocky precipice. The boy watched them remove some spit of stalk from their pockets and thoughtfully chew upon these.

The man leaned upon his rifle and with his free hand turned the woman's head about so that she was suddenly looking up into his face and the rain. She gave a silent moan; her face was slick with mud and ravaged by a terrible swelling. He lowered his face and said something to her. She keened softly and closed her eyes.

The boy crouched down, hands circling his knees. He was looking with fascination at the three prisoners. The isolated pools of water had now become one large pool of muddy, gushing water, eroding the soil and chewing away at the lip of this small plateau, with the result that the three bodies were ever so slowly sliding down the incline, their boots now all but touching the edge of the cliff. They would soon tumble to their deaths in the great valley below.

The man knelt by the boy, also absorbed in this phenomenon.

"Kolooltopec?" the man said to the boy.

"Yes."

"Kolooltopec, which does not exist?"

"Yes?"

"How is it that a Toodoo boy from Moogradi has come to be in the company of these crazy people in journey towards Kolooltopec?"

"I am their guide."

"Then you are not the best of guides or you would have known not to come by way of this jurisdiction."

"Yes."

"My officers are much disturbed."

"Yes."

"It has occurred to them that you and these gringos may be spies."

The boy regarded the officers in silence. They were at first few in number, now there were numerous, all assembled under the small protection of the rocky overhang, chewing on whatever dried meat or vine they had to chew upon, and jabbering softly among themselves.

"Are you spies?"

The boys reached into the puddle at his feet, and pitched a small stone out over the valley.

The woman had risen to her hands and knees. They watched her hold to that position; she seemed unempowered to do more. One of her companions let out a helpless moan as water coursed about him and slid him another few inches out over the cliff.

"A Toodoo does not spy," the boy said.

"No. He only journeys towards what does not exist."

The officers under the small overhang had broken off twigs from a nearby bush, and were now comparing them for length. The longest was perhaps two inches. The shortest could barely be seen.

The man turned on his heels and made a gesture towards them. "How long before our unfortunate prisoners hurtle to their deaths?"

The officers displayed their various sticks. They were jabbering and laughing among themselves. The rain had momentarily slackened; it now drove down again in a renewed burst.

The prisoner nearest the edge gave a strangled cry.

The boy touched the officer's arm.

"They have a map," he said.

"Oh?"

"A map which purports to show where Kolooltopec may be found."

The man considered this statement. He rubbed his eyes and wiped both hands across his face. The boy noticed that the skin on the man's hands was deeply scarred and that none of his fingers were longer than his thumbs. They had been cut away, the boy thought, probably with an axe.

"'Purports,'" the man said. "I do not know this word. What does it mean, this 'purports,' and how does it come to pass that a boy from Moogradi makes use of the unknown word?"

"School," the boy said. "I was a student."

"Ah. So the famous Moogradi village now has a school?"

"My village once had school. But the teacher vanished and the school was torched."

The man nodded.

"And did your great village have a fine clinic where the sick could come?"

"Yes."

"Which was also torched? So that now your clinic and school and the schoolteacher, along with the Frooloo family you have never heard of, is lost to the world? Does not exist? Like our fabled Kolooltopec?"

"Yes."

"But your adventurers have a map, you say?"

"Yes."

A couple of the soldiers ventured out from their overhang and dragged the two male prisoners a few feet forward from the cliff edge.

"You have seen this map?"

"Many times. They have studied it unceasingly."

"'Unceasingly'?"

"Yes."

"It this map a good map?"

The boy shook his head. "It is a worthless map. It is a map to Kolooltopec."

"I wish to see this map."

"Of course."

They sat in their crouch, side by side, for some while before saying anything further.

"Which of these fine prisoners possesses the valueless document?"

The boy pointed at the woman. She sat folded over, her head at droop on her knees.

She had cropped her hair close to her skull the second day out from the village; the boy had some of this woman's shorn hair still in his pocket.

"Does this prisoner, who possesses the famous map, also possess a name?"

"They call her Emma."

"Emma. I have never known anyone purporting to possess this name."

The boy shrugged.

"Has Emma been good to the guide from Moogradi?" asked the man. He circled one hand lazily over his groin.

The boy grinned.

"Unceasingly."

The officers under the protection of the overhang laughed merrily. Some few of them now had their shirts off. They would step out into the warm rain for a few minutes, wash themselves, and then step back into their drier environment. Then they would step out into the rain again and for a few brief seconds furiously scrub and flap their ragged shirts. The boy studied these half-naked officers. He could count their ribs. One had a filthy cloth wrapping his chest; the blood flowed red for a second, then went pinkish in the rain, before the red stain showed again. Another of these officers was a boy not much older than himself. He tried catching this one's eyes, although it was clear the young officer had no interest in one of his experience. Several of them were women. The soldiers now numbered a dozen or more, a fresh face frequently arriving, although the boy could not see how this was possible unless they had burrowed a tunnel somewhere through the mountain and its mouth was nearby.

"Where are these crazy people from?" the man asked.

"America."

The man weighed this, watching the woman. He seemed amused.

"I had a young cousin who went to live in the country of America. Perhaps I and these prisoners are related."

The boy smiled halfheartedly. "I hope your cousin in America is well," he said.

"I thank you for your good wishes. But I expect this young cousin is now dead. He returned home, you see."

"It grieves me to hear it."

"I thank you. Yes, he is dead. My village was not so fortunate as your Moogradi with its teacher and clinic and the vanished school."

The boy shut his eyes.

"But I have my officers and it is not wise to dwell upon those sorrowful deaths."

The boy was crying. But he reasoned that no one would notice in the falling rain.

The woman had moved again. She had crawled in the mud to a spot somewhat removed from her two companions. She lay with her head between two large rocks, her muddy hands covering her head.

The rain had turned cold. The sky was darkening.

It seemed to the boy that there now were as many as twenty officers milling about the tiny encampment.

"These crazy people," asked the man. "Do they have food?"

"Yes."

"Is it good?"

"Yes. Although it is of a kind I have never tasted before. They call it hiking food."

"Hiking food? You are right. I have never heard of hiking food."

The officers were busy under their little overhang. They were on their hands and knees working with knives and sticks and an assortment of other tools. They were enlarging their little pocket in the mountainside.

"Tell me this," the officer said to the boy. "In your five days' journey towards Kolooltopec did you come across soldiers wearing the uniform of our republic?"

"Yes. In their camp at the headwaters. But they let us continue when your prisoners showed them their documents, and after prolonged inquiry."

"Because you were on your way to Kolooltopec, which does not exist."

The boy shrugged.

"Which meant that our prisoners were not to be taken seriously?"

"Yes."

"Or perhaps your three friends are peacekeepers from the famous United Nations, and the soldiers of the republic did not wish to offend their benefactors."

"I do not know."

"And because the soldiers of the republic were given money."

"Yes."

"And what was the view of the soldiers of the republic as to the merits of the boy from Moogradi?"

"I do not know."

"My officers have heard there are informers in Moogradi. Some, so it is reported, express sympathy for the cause of the soldiers of the republic, while others align themselves with our movement. The Frooloo family, for instance. Have you heard these reports?"

"I have heard whispers."

"Did these soldiers of the republic harm you?"

"Not excessively."

"What does this mean, this 'not excessively'?"

"They twisted my arms. They beat me about the head."

"But not excessively."

"No."

"Since I see no visible wounds."

"Yes. No." The boy was confused.

"No cigarettes to your skin. No finger in the electrical socket. No axe to your hand or your head in the vice. No threats to put the torch to the whole of your wonderful Moogradi as you and your family are asleep on your mats."

"No."

"Because you were the guide for these people from the country of America who are now my prisoners and not because you are a spy in the employment of these soldiers of the republic?"

"Yes."

One of the officers strode over and slapped the boy hard in the face. The boy tumbled into the mud, and lay still until the man who said he was Raoul helped him to his feet.

"You will excuse him," he said. "My officers are distrustful of boy guides from Moogradi. He thinks you have been making a count of our members."

The boy looked at the coursing ground. His shoulders were shaking.

"How many would you estimate are among us?"

"I do not know." The boy took a deep sigh and squared his shoulders. He looked into his inquisitor's eyes. "It was out of curiosity only. But your officers seem to come and go."

The man smiled sadly. He lay his hand over the backside of the boy, and said, "Yes. Yes. I agree. They come and they go."

"I am sorry," the boy said.

"Yes, we are all sorry." He held the boy's cheek in the hand with the shorn fingers, and lifted the boy's head into the rain. "Look up there," he said.

The boy squinted his eyes and looked up into the cold rain. The mountains here stretched another ten thousand feet, but the sky was all but black now and the boy could see nothing of that vast height in the blinding rain.

"We are as numerous as the raindrops," the man said. "That is how many." The man allowed him to lower his face, and affectionately tousled the boy's hair. The officers wove in and out. The boy was now convinced they had burrowed some crawl space through the mountain. But it would have taken them many years to accomplish this; perhaps the task was begun even before he was born. The war had been going on a long time.

The man and the boy watched as the two male prisoners rose and staggered over to the rocks and dropped down into a heap near where the woman was lying.

"Why are they so spiritless?" the man asked the boy. "We have not harmed them."

The boy peered at his thin ankles puddled in the muddy, streaming water. "No, you did not harm them. But they did not believe it would be so difficult as this, reaching Kolootopec."

"Then they are crazy."

"Yes. They are crazy."

The woman seemed to be trying to scramble away from the two men, but her feet kept sliding from beneath her as rainwater sluiced its trails down the mountain. There was no place she could go, in any event.

Some of the officers were still digging into the mountainside. Others were laboriously attempting to get a fire going beneath a teepee of small, smoking sticks erected within a ring of stones.

The boy found he had fallen asleep, because when he opened his eyes the man was shaking him.

"My prisoners whom you are guiding to Kolooltopec, do they have money? How is it they are funding this elusive expedition?"

"I do not know. They are very strange on the subject."

"In what manner?"

"They bargained long hours with my family before my fee could be settled. They feared they might be cheated."

"What was the settlement, may I ask?"

"My family received one thousand moolees. A second thousand is to be paid upon my safe return."

The man's face brightened. "Two thousand? Two thousand moolees is very little. Such a sum, I believe, would amount to no more than ten or so of your friend Emma's American dollars."

"Yes. But since the Koo does not exist then the expedition to it is foolish and thus has no value. So my family did not wish to charge extravagantly for my services."

"Agreed. But there is still the issue of your time and expertise. Do you know the word, 'expertise'?"

"Yes."

"Or there might also be the extra remuneration to your family for the small informational services you are meant to provide the soldiers of the republic."

"No."

The man smiled and playfully ruffled the boy's hair. The boy shivered.

"On the other hand, you are serving your explorers as guide through a terrain totally unknown to yourself. Do you agree?"

"Yes."

"So the sum of two thousand moolees is perhaps fair."

"Yes. Such was my family's determination after long delibera-tion of the matter, and after much imbibing of the pulqoo."

"Ah, the pulqoo! Did your adventurers admire the pulqoo?"

"They became very merry. They could not stand up. The woman said she would return once she found Kolooltopec, and marry any handsome man in my village who could provide her with an eternal flow of the pulqoo."

"She said this!"

"Many times."

They looked admiringly over at the woman. She was holding a flat wedge of slate over her head, this slate providing shelter of a sort, under which her downcast face was hidden by multiple curtains of rain and a fine mist now steaming up from the earth.

"Yes, many times," the boy said. "But the next day she repented."

He pulled the woman's wet hair out from his pocket and showed it to this man who might or might not be the legendary figure Raoul.

The hair was examined at length although the man would not touch it.

"Did the soldiers of the republic do this to our Emma?"

"No. She clipped the hair herself because of the heat."

"It was not the best hair, to begin with."

"No. It is not the best hair."

Finally he was told to return the woman's hair to his pocket, and the boy quickly complied.

"And our other prisoners, what did they do under influence of the pulqoo?"

"They argued and shouted. They danced and sang."

"As did your own people?"

"Yes."

"And how is it your poor family in the insolvent village of Moogradi chanced to have such a wealth of the wonderful pulqoo?"

"The jugs had been hidden, along with my sisters, when the soldiers of the republic occupied our village. It did not take much pulqoo to arouse the enthusiasm of our distinguished visitors."

"My officers would give much to have this pulqoo in front of them this minute."

The officers who heard this left off their digging and fire building to shout out "Pulqoo, pulqoo," while thrusting their arms time and time again into the air.

"But alas," the man said. "Alas, the pulqoo is all hidden away in

Moogradi, side by side with its young daughters."

"Alas."

The officers had succeeded in getting a fire going. It was a high blaze now, with thick smoke pummeling above the flames and vanishing moments later within the ceaseless rain.

"Excuse me," the officer said.

The woman's head was down between her bent knees, her shoulders scrunched. She looked up, startled, when his hands touched her. He said something to her, and the boy, incomprehensibly, heard her laugh. The man helped her to her feet and led her over to the fire. One of the many officers milling about there dislodged a large stone and rolled it up by the fire. The man seated her upon the stone and after a moment her face lifted and she held her hands up to the fire. Several officers thrust their little spits of food upon her, but this she refused.

The other two prisoners arose and staggered towards the assembly.

The man returned and stood by the boy, who had given up trying to follow the movements of the officers and could no longer even guess at their numbers.

"We will first warm them," the man said. "Perhaps then we will shoot them."

"The Toodoo family thanks you in their behalf."

"On the other hand, if my officers shoot them the Toodoo family of Moogradi will be denied their next one thousand moolees and our adventurers will never reach Kolooltopec."

"They will not reach it in any case."

The boy's eyes snapped open. For a moment he had imagined he saw doors opening in the mountainside and a stream of officers, endless in number, entering and leaving.

The man knelt beside him.

"These soldiers of the republic, in their garrison at the headwaters, were they many?"

"No more than fifty."

"Well-armed?"

"Yes. With heavy weapons, including artillery. Many trucks, and armored vehicles without number."

"Yes. More vehicles than they have soldiers to fill them. But such vehicles cannot scale these mountains. Are they well-fed?"

"They have much food, and more cargo arriving by the hour."

"Which cargo they will not distribute among the people for whom it is intended. Is this correct?"

The boy spat into the mud at his feet.

"These goods are stamped in what manner?"

"The usual."

The man was quiet for some time.

The boy heard some little noise from afar and thought he saw a trip of goats at graze beyond the clearing.

He closed his eyes, hugging himself against the rain.

It was a very cold rain now, and he could not stop his limbs from shaking; his buttocks were all but numb in the icy, flowing water, and a wind was whipping the rain against his face. He had his shoulders turned towards the fire and he imagined he could feel some little heat against the skin.

"And what did these heros of the republic say to you of my officers?"

"They were contemptuous. Raoul's forces were puny, and cowardly, and beneath consideration, they said. His officers were of diminished capacity, without weaponry, the daughters of rodents, and were at final rot in the jungle. The insurrection would soon be terminated, they said, and your heads afloat in the river."

"Yes. Yet they are frightened and dare not venture outside their garrisons, except to pillage and burn innocent villages, and rape and maim our sisters. What is the news of the latest atrocity?"

"We saw fresh burning along the river. The villagers at the headwaters spoke of many corpses. Some say it is the work of your officers. Most believe otherwise."

The officer unslung his rifle, yanked back the bolt, and showed the boy his rifle's empty chamber. He stroked the wet stock before returning the weapon to his shoulder.

"Lamentable, yes?" he said. "But do not surmise from this deficiency that we are unempowered."

The boy did not speak of that other matter of which he had heard whispered speculation, even within the household of the Toodoo family of Moogradi: of the many villages, up and down river, largely deserted now. Of the great secret exodus of his people to a sanctuary high in these mountains.

"My teacher spoke of Raoul's cause with much reverence."

"He who has vanished."

"Yes."

"And is likely rotting in the jungle."

"Yes. Or his head afloat in the river."

"Perhaps your scholar has found bliss in Kolooltopec."

"That is doubtful."

"I agree. That is all but impossible. But your friends, you say, have with them a map."

"Yes. It is wrapped in skin inside the woman's pocket."

"In Emma's pocket. And what is in the pockets of her companions? Money? Tobacco? Beads? The pulqoo?"

"I do not know. They have a card."

"A card?"

"Yes. A gold card."

"A card made of gold? I do not believe it. For what purpose?"

"I am uncertain. They took their gold card to the bank in Foolderoo and came out with a fistful of our moolees, one thousand of which they presented to my family. I saw this with my own eyes."

"I must see this card of gold."

"Of course."

"And the map."

"Naturally."

"My officers are expert readers of maps."

"Yes."

"And we know the country."

"Precisely."

"You do not think our presence would diminish your own guide's assignment?"

"Quite the contrary."

"A thousand such maps distributed wisely along the river might prove profitable for those hidden away beside your pulqoo."

"Yes. If Kolooltopec exists."

"But it does not exist."

"No. Even so, the woman asleep by the fire has the map."

"Yes. Perhaps we should join her."

"If you are satisfied a boy from Moogradi deserves this honor."

"I cannot attest to the boy's honor. But I will extend to you our welcome."

"I am grateful."

They could see steam rising from the flesh of the three outsiders, and their wet clothes smoking. Some few other fires were alight now and the officers, some thirty or more, huddled around these, on this craggy lip of mountain.

For a moment the rain thinned and the boy thought he saw a thousand faces strung out over the hillside, and fires from a string of other such encampments carved into the mountainside; in these could be seen the stark faces of mothers nursing their babies, and old women tending the fire pots; he could see bony children of his own age and younger at kneel upon the stone shelves, and goats, and pigs, and burros, and an ancient, bedraggled figure with hollow eyes seated upon a bird cage.

But he blinked and shook his head and when his eyes cleared they had all vanished. There was only loud, coursing water, and great sheets of rain splattering like gunshots all about them.

The boy slumbered by the fire, his body at rest among the three adventurers for whom he was guide. He was thinking of the one thousand moolees paid and of the one thousand more his family in Moogradi would likely never receive, since Kolooltopec was only a figment of the crazy imagination.

He slept. Then it was morning, and blinding sunlight, and the earth already baking, and considerable activity in their encampment.

"Onwards," the officers were shouting. "Onwards to Koolooltopec!"

Up and down the mountainside came the same cry. "Onwards. Onwards to Kolooltopec!"

A Male in the Women's Locker Room

is a shoe in the refrigerator,
a mouse in the oven. Five years old,
already a Y chromosome. No, that's not fair,

I don't know that he's a boy
from the bare chest, short hair—
s/he could be her mother's experiment,

like Hemingway. One doesn't have to be a boy
to shoot lions, shirtless, lean with cool aplomb
against the jeep. But how else could he have learned

to kick the stall door hiding his mother,
to move through space as if he owned it,
his solid body absorbing molecules of oxygen

like M&M's. With his pudgy baby hands,
his skin like talcum, he's too young
for an Adam's apple, though his neck

shows promise. Of what? Not ice dancing.
Maybe it's not that he's male but that he's clothed
in navy trunks and I'm just about

to pull off my things. I could go to a stall,
but he's only five. So I strip.
He doesn't crack a smile—what's it like in those joints

with a cover charge and tips? Now his mother's doing
makeup in the mirror; she doesn't see
the way he's watching me, now stark naked. He peers

across the bench, the scientist dismantling DNA;
I'm a goat in a petting zoo.
He takes in my breasts and pubic hair;

it's all her fault. That's mean, he's only five;
she couldn't park him like a car. But no father
would bring his daughter to look

at naked men. If this were Europe, would I care?
The Pilgrims carried modesty like syphilis;
in Sweden he'd have seen so many naked women,

I doubt he'd stare. At three, he'd be cute,
like an animal. At least he's not ten, or twenty-two.
Then, I let myself think what I would do:

run or scream. Here, I'm three times his size.
I could break his wrists like chopsticks.

DEAN YOUNG

Ready-Made Bouquet

It's supposed to be spring but the sky
might as well be a huge rock floating
in the sky. I'm the guy who always forgets

to turn his oven off pre-heat but I might
as well be the one with the apple in front
of his face or the one with Botticelli's
Flora hovering at his back, scattering

her unlikely flowers. Which is worse?
To have your vision forever blocked or
forever to miss what everyone else can
see, the beautiful *Kick me* sign hanging
from your back? Is there anything more

ridiculous than choosing between despairs?
Part of me is still standing in the falling

snow with my burning chicken. In a black slip,
a woman despairs in front of her closet
five minutes before the guests arrive.
In the tub, a man sobs, trying to reread
a letter that's turning to mush. Despair

of rotten fruit, bruised fruit. Despair
of having a bad cat, garbage strewn over
your shoes, sofa in shreds. Despair of saying,
You bet I hate to get rid of him but I'm
joining the Peace Corps, to the girl who
calls about the ad. The despair of realizing

despair may be a necessary precondition

of joy which complicates your every thought
just as someone screaming in the hall, Get
away from me, complicates the lecture on
Wallace Stevens. Ghostlier demarcations,
keener sounds. Wallace Stevens causes despair

for anyone trying to write poems or a book
called *Wallace Stevens and the Interpersonal.*
Sometimes interpersonal despair may lead to
a lengthy critical project's completion but how

could Jessica leave me in 1973 after pledging
those things in bed, after the afternoon looking
at Magrittes? The tuba on fire. The bottle with
breasts. Didn't I wander the streets half the night,

hanging out at the wharf, afraid of getting beat up
just to forget that one kiss in front of the bio-
morphic shape with the sign saying *Sky* in French?
The stone table and stone loaf of bread. The room

filled with a rose. Loving someone who doesn't
love you may lead to writing impenetrable poems
and/or staying awake until dawn, drawn to airy,
azure behaviors of gulls and spaceships.
Some despairs may be relieved by other despairs

as in not knowing how to pay for psychoanalysis,
as in wrecking your car, as in this poem. Please
pass me another quart of kerosene. A cygnet
is a baby swan. Hatrack, cheese cake, mold.
The despair of wading through a river at night

towards a cruel lover is powerfully evoked
in Chekhov's story "Agafya." The heart seems
designed for despair especially if you study
embryology while being in love with your lab

partner who lets you kiss her under the charts
of organelles but doesn't respond although

later you think she didn't not respond either
which fills you with idiotic hope very like
despair just as a cloud can be very like
a cannon, the way it starts out as a simple
tube then ties itself into a knot. The heart,
I mean. It seems, for Magritte, many things

that are not cannons may be called cannons
to great effect. David's despair is ongoing
and a lot like his father's, currently treated
with drugs that may cause disorientation and

hair loss. Men in white coats run from
the burning asylum. No, wait, it's not burning,
it's not an asylum, it's a parking lot
in sunset and they want you to pay. Sometimes
Rick thinks Nancy joined the Peace Corps just

to get away from him so later he joins the Peace Corps
to get away from someone else, himself it turns out,
and wades into a river where tiny, spiny fish
dart up your penis if you piss while in the river.
Don't piss while in the river is a native saying

he thinks at first is symbolic. The despair
of loving may lead to long plane rides with
little leg room, may lead to a penis full
of fish, a burning chicken, a room filled

with a single, pink rose. Funny, how
we think of it as a giant rose,
not a tiny room.

The Mother Explains the Father to the Son

He will tell you how each day wears the impress
of childhood fields, where he was made to
kneel and harvest darkness, then extract
its most pure element, which his father
used on his mother with rags, like
chloroform. This is the most you will get.
He has no notch or opening primed for
release, no pulling away of edges. Though
you might accidentally witness the
secret and ominous cleansing—the suppressed
purge. The same way the sky sometimes
seeps a misery of rain, like fever.
It is then that you will not be able to turn away.
There is something hypnotic where
anguish puts down its bed.
He will be careful with you. Not the way
clouds are with pond surfaces,
but in the way that says pain does not
exist if it is not perceived. This is how he
will protect you. I have forgotten the long-ago
night kisses, their sensation; but not the
cobalt glass bottles lining his father's porch
railing. Each night they collected lake dew and
distillate of moon, then colluded with the heat
of the morning sun in the perfect crime of
undoing, as if the night, the dew,
everything involved had been an illusion,
a slight of some elemental hand.

Another Life

"That was in another life," we say.
Everyone knows what that means—
another love, in another country.
"In another life, when I drank chartreuse,
densely herbal, fresh green on my tongue,
the light filtering through new rainwater
fell on a face, beside a café window...."
I hear about another's other life
which seems happier than the other lives
I've led—how could I have been
the one that led those other lives?
A few sprigs of green at Christmastime,
no tree. I'd put lights on the schefflera,
open some wine, secretly listen to the Festival
of Lessons and Carols on the radio,
in another life dreaming of another life.
Now I am in the life I dreamed of,
or am I? The borders of the world
are still lit with gold, uncertain radiance,
shimmering beyond the wing of the airplane,
or over the lip of a glass. Someone's other life
flickers in his eyes, still beautiful,
closed off, complete. When he looks up
he looks at me as if I were a stranger
looking at him as if he were a stranger.

Monet's Olympia

She reclines, more or less.
Try that posture, it's hardly languor.
Her right arm sharp angles.
With her left she conceals her ambush.
Shoes but not stockings,
how sinister. The flower
behind her ear is naturally
not real, of a piece
with the sofa's drapery.
The windows (if any) are shut.
This is indoor sin.
Above the head of the (clothed) maid
is an invisible voice balloon: *Slut.*

But. Consider the body,
unfragile, defiant, the pale nipples
staring you right in the bull's-eye.
Consider also the black ribbon
around the neck. What's under it?
A fine red threadline, where the head
was taken off and glued back on.
The body's on offer,
but the neck's as far as it goes.
This is no morsel.
Put clothes on her and you'd have a schoolteacher,
the kind with the brittle whiphand.

There's someone else in this room.
You, Monsieur Voyeur.
As for that object of yours
she's seen those before, and better.

I, the head, am the only subject
of this picture.
You, Sir, are furniture.
Get stuffed.

Uchepas

Tamales plain-steamed then whitened
like a wedding dress with cream
and *queso*. A beautiful simple food.
And not enough. We want more.

We are cravers of storms and *choques*
on the highway. We never mind
waiting in the long stopped lines
if at the end there can be some blood.

Forget our lovers. We want
a stranger, shiver deepest at the
hairs on the backs of someone's
hands, who has not touched us yet.

Five Years Ago

It was Labor Day, September 2, a Monday, five years ago, and I was twenty-seven years old and about to bring my forty-four-year-old mother and my forty-four-year-old father together for the first time in my adult life. All my life I had daydreamed about this moment, wondered if it would ever happen, and now that it was about to happen, I was so emotional, I was almost out of control. The night before, my father had flown into Chicago from Boston, where he worked as a real estate broker. He was staying, like the last time, at his mother's house. I drove down to his mother's on Fifty-fifth and Indiana Avenue to pick him up. Mother Zoe—that's what I call his mother, my grandmother—was sitting at the kitchen table with her cup of coffee when I knocked on the back door and there was my father—whom I hadn't seen but once before—two years earlier when he came back to Chicago, that time, I think, because a brokers' convention was being held in Chicago. He was slender and brown and handsome and wore a beard and was smiling at me as I came in. Apparently ready to go, he was already holding a tan summer jacket across his arm. I blushed and felt something like a current of electricity shoot through my body as I simply lowered my head, hiding my joy, and walked straight over to him and slid my arms under his and around his body—which fitted mine nicely—and hugged him for all I was worth. I knew I was going to cry. Tears were already rimming my eyes. All it would take was a blink. And I wanted my face over his shoulder, so I'd be looking out the kitchen window, my back to Mother Zoe, when the tears came. But it didn't help and finally it didn't matter. I not only cried but I sobbed, sobbed with joy and pain and love for this man I'd dreamed of and fearfully wondered about all my life. And here he was. Two years before, I had expected him to appear suddenly bigger than life, but when I came into Mother Zoe's house that time and saw him sitting at the dining room table with his

mother, with his elbows on the table, he seemed so small, so fragile, so frail, compared to the giant I'd imagined. He was just a
flesh and blood human being, a man, and one not especially
imposing, just an ordinary man. But that time I didn't rush to
him and hug him. I was too confused, too scared. He stood up
and came to me and hugged me, put his arms around me and
kissed my forehead. And, yes, that time, too, I cried. I cried but I
pulled away in embarrassment, pulled back and went and sat
down beside Mother Zoe, who patted me on my thigh. I was
wearing jeans. I remember. Jeans and a blouse. And my curly hair
was pulled back. I hadn't known how to dress for him. Before
going down to Mother Zoe's, I'd tried on four different dresses
and six pairs of shoes and finally rejected all of them and pulled
on a pair of jeans and told my husband, Austin, "If my father
can't accept me in jeans, then, then—" but I couldn't finish the
sentence. And I remember my husband—who, by the way, is ten
years older than my father—saying, "Don't worry. He'll be happy
to see you." But, you know, I was never quite sure that he was.
Something about him seemed guarded. I'm still talking about
that first time two years before. Sure, he hugged me but it was a
stiff hug. Maybe he was nervous, too. Maybe it was simply that he
didn't know what to expect and was maybe even a little bit scared
of me. Yes, that's what I felt. Felt that he was scared of me. After
all, he hadn't seen me since, since... Well, actually, I don't think
he ever saw me after two or three. And I don't remember him at
all. I know from what Mother told me. They took him to court,
you know. Tried to force him to marry or support her. But my
mother, Pandora, was only sixteen. And my father, Barry Stanton,
was exactly sixteen, too. Both of them still in high school. Mess-
ing around, they got me. And got themselves in a world of trouble. In fact, Mother got thrown out of school and Father joined
the Army. Mother's family said he ran away from his responsibility. That's the way they saw it. But I was talking about that first
time seeing him and comparing it to seeing him this time. And
this time I just walked right over to him and put my arms around
him and he didn't feel like a stranger anymore. And I had gotten
this fantasy version of him, this giant of a man, down to size. I
was just hugging my father, just a normal human being, a man, a

handsome man with a face like mine. I could see myself in his face. Looking into his eyes, in a wonderfully strange way, gave me myself in a new way for the first time. I felt so close to him it was almost terrifying. When I hugged him I felt his heart beating against my breast and I held him close just to continue feeling his rhythm. Tears running down my cheeks, sobbing, I held him long and hard. But I started shaking and I pulled back and said, "I'm sorry, I'm sorry—" but I couldn't bring myself to call him Daddy or Father. I also couldn't call him Barry, just plain Barry. I didn't know what to call him. Anyway, the plan was he'd have breakfast, no, brunch, with Pandora—his old high school girlfriend—and my husband, Austin, and my sister, Yvette, and my six-year-old daughter, Octavia, and me. Mother Zoe was still in her bathrobe, with her gray hair kind of standing out every whichaway. And just as we were leaving Winona came down the hall into the kitchen and said, "Now, Ophelia, when are you bringing Barry back? You know we got plans for this afternoon?" And something in Winona's tone offended me but I held back and refused to lash out although I wanted to. He was *my* father. I had spent twenty-seven years without him and here was his sister—who grew up with him, who had visited him more than once in Boston—telling me to cut my time with him short, bring him back, don't hog his time. I got so pissed I could have screamed but I didn't. I just looked at Winona standing there in her bathrobe with the corners of her big pretty mouth turned up like she was expecting me to give her trouble. And Mother Zoe jumped in and said, "That's right. And I sure hope you ain't planning to have your mother over there. I told you not to invite her. Didn't I?" And I couldn't remember Mother Zoe making such a request or demand till she said, "Remember, I said, just you and Barry, quiet brunch together with you and your husband and your daughter. Just to get to know your father." Then I remembered but I hadn't taken her words to imply that Mother wasn't to be invited. And anyway, what was this thing about, anyway? Mother Zoe hated my mother from the beginning, from the time she came home from work unexpectedly and caught Mother and her son making love on the couch. Mother told me all about it. Mother Zoe drove her out, shouting at her, calling her a whore, a tramp, a cheap little bitch. No woman, Mother said, was ever good enough for Mother Zoe's son. Mother said she thought he would turn into a faggot—her word—the situation was so bad. But why now all these years later did I have to be the victim of this shit, the victim of these ill feelings that existed between Mother Zoe and sixteen-year-old Pandora Lowell years ago? Why did the mess present itself just when I wanted more than anything in the world to bring my mother and father together and feel, for the first time, like I had a real family? So, I didn't say anything. I just nodded. I assured Winona I'd get her brother back before noon. And my father and I left. Octavia was waiting in the car in the back seat. And while we drove south—I live at Ninety-fifth and Yates—I had the warmest feeling listening to my father talking with my daughter. He was asking her about her school, about what she liked to do, and being the smart kid she was, she kept telling him about a spelling contest she'd just won, and about her winning in the girl's footrace, and about her great math scores. They seemed to hit it off better this time than they had the first time when she was four. Back then she wasn't really that interested in him. But now she had a great curiosity because she had been made to feel his importance. Some kids had grandfathers, others didn't. In a way, it had become very important to her in the last year or so to have a grandfather. Having one—at least at her school, Martin R. Delany School, the best private school on the South Side—was a status symbol, especially since so many kids there don't. In fact, I had encouraged her to write to him in Boston and she did send him three or four letters but he answered only once, and only with a postcard. I had to reassure her that her grandfather loved her—though I didn't believe it, didn't even believe he loved me, his own daughter—and that he was simply too busy to spare time to write often. Anyway, when we got to the house my sister, Yvette, was in the kitchen working on the muffins. She makes great blueberry muffins. We could smell them the minute I turned off the motor and the smell got stronger as we walked up the back walkway from the garage, and while crossing the patio, I slid my arm around my father's waist and hugged him to me. My father, I thought, my father, here with me. And I quickly kissed his cheek. And the minute we stepped up onto the back porch there was Mother sitting in one of the straw chairs waiting. And I thought of Mother Zoe and her warning and all I could hope was that my father would not tell. This was the moment. I had brought these two together for the first time since they were teenagers. I think the last time they saw each other was in a courtroom when they both were eighteen, and Mother was trying to get some money out of him, just before he joined the Army and disappeared. But this was the big moment now. The one I had waited for. This was my moment. The three of us stood there. Octavia walked between us into the house and into the kitchen, following the smell of blueberry muffins. I watched my father and Mother just looking at each other, looking fearfully. There was a distance of about five feet between them. He was trying to smile. God only knows what he was thinking. He didn't look happy to see her. In fact, he seemed a bit irritated. And she was giving him this cynical sideways look she can get. It's a half sneer. I've seen it all my life. Then she did something she no doubt thought was a smile but it really didn't come out right. It was more a grimace. But she sort of slung her string bean of a body over to him and for a split second I thought she was going to hug him, thought he was going to respond by hugging her, but that's not what happened. She grabbed his beard and tugged at it forcefully, yanked it back and forth, and her mouth was twisted in an agonizing grin and her eyes were blazing with contempt, though she was trying to laugh and to be playful. I'm sure she meant the gesture to be playful but it didn't come off that way at all. She yanked him too hard and he frowned and stepped back a couple of paces, pulling away from her. And she was saying, "What is this crap on your face?" And he was beginning to sneer. I saw just the edge of his canine. An almost imperceptible shudder moved through his face—his cheeks and his chin especially, and his eyes, like her own, blazed. And I wondered why I myself was feeling so elated, so up, so complete—for the first time—and why at the same time everything was obviously going wrong. These two people, I could see, should never have been brought together. Not only did they not like each other, they held contempt for each other. And though I had known that to be the case I hadn't wanted to know it. And it gave me for the first time in my life a clear sense of the emotional foundation of my life. But even then, sensing this then, I didn't want to face it, didn't want the full sense of it to reach my conscience. So I ignored it, pretended the hostility between them was not serious, not important, that, in fact, there was something deeper that held them together and that something was me, my presence in the world. Like it or not, I was their link. And I wanted them to like it. Oh, I so desperately wanted them to like it. So, grabbing Mother by the sleeve and my father by his elbow, I pulled them toward the kitchen, saying, "Come on, let's see what's cooking." And in the kitchen there was my sister and my husband and my daughter. My sister turned around from the stove as I introduced her to my father, Barry Stanton, and she reached out, smiling, and shook his hand. Yvette is a very pretty girl, with bright red full lips, yellowish green eyes, tall and slender with naturally reddish hair, a hair color unusual for a colored girl. (People say we look alike. It's because we both look like Mother, whose hair is also red.) My sister was twenty-three then. And men were after her like crazy. In fact, she said, "I invited Robert over for brunch. Hope you guys don't mind." And though I resented the liberty she'd taken, I held back saying anything. Then my husband, Austin, standing in the doorway watching my father meet my sister, was smiling. Austin is such an elegant gentleman. He was nearing retirement, early retirement at that time. He was fifty-five and had been head of his own law firm, Tate, Jones and Bedford, on Seventy-third and Cottage Grove, for the last fifteen years. He was now financially secure and wanted to stop work so he could go fishing when he felt like it, so he could be with his young daughter more and with me, too. Although he and I hadn't been getting along all that well lately, I still respected and liked him. He was like a father to me. In fact, it's true, he had raised me, in a way. Taught me a lot. As he put it, he had made a "lady" out of me, sent me to law school and given me a comfortable middle-class life in a good South Side neighborhood. I now had a position in his firm and I was holding my own. And after passing the bar last year I defended my first client in a civil case, a woman fighting for child support. I was saying, "Austin Tate, my husband, meet Barry Stanton, my father," and I sounded awkward but the moment seemed grand to me and I felt that a certain formality was needed. Now, my husband and my father were shaking hands and gazing into each other's eyes with tentative kindness. And at least their meeting was going well. Then Austin said, "Welcome to our home. How does it feel to be back in Chicago?" and my father was saying something but I was no longer listening to him because Yvette was having an emergency with the omelettes she was making, breaking eggs into a big enamel bowl, she'd come across a bad egg, and she'd cried out as though bitten by a snake or as though she'd burned her hand on the hot stove, and I turned to her to help. And Mother all this time stood in the doorway between the kitchen and the back porch watching, I sensed, with a lingering though slight expression of contempt. And Octavia ran her finger around in the blueberry batter bowl, then, with her eyes closed in bliss, licked the finger. And I said, "By the way, we're eating out on the patio. It's nice out there this time of morning. You guys go on out," I said with a wave of the hand, "and get started, I want to get my camera, and show my father my office." And I took him by the hand and pulled him up the hall, then up the narrow stair to the second floor where Austin's and my and Octavia's bedrooms were. And I led him into my little study at the back of the house. A place I was proud of. My law diploma was framed on the wall over my desk and I wanted him to see it. But I wasn't planning to point his nose in that direction. But I did stand with my back to my desk—my camera was there on the desk—and took my father by both of his hands and pulled him to me, so that he would be facing—over my shoulders—the vivid evidence of my accomplishment. Three things I was proud of, this degree, my career, and my daughter. And I wanted my father to admire me for those three accomplishments. So I pulled him against my belly and put my arms around him and held him close so that our bodies were breathing together. Thinking back on that moment I know it was a strange thing to do, but I felt so close to him, needed to be so close to him, and wanted him to feel what I was feeling. Touching him this way was the only way I knew how to reach him. Then I kissed him, fully on the mouth and forced my tongue into his mouth, kissed him the way I kissed my husband, kissed him deeply, so deeply he would have to feel how passionately I loved him, how deeply I felt for him, how much he meant to me. I held his head with one hand and held his back with the other and I lifted my stomach toward him and pressed harder and harder, and I felt him respond, felt his whole body come alive in my arms. Then I slowly let him go and nodded toward my diploma, and said, "See? I earned that all by myself." And he took his glasses out of his jacket pocket and put them on and read the words, actually read the words, read them slowly, then he said, "I'm very proud of you, Ophelia." And I squeezed his hand. Then he said, "We have so much to talk about. I wish there was time—" and I said, "Now that we've found each other, there will be endless time. I want to know everything, everything you've ever felt and done, *everything*." And while he looked a little embarrassed by my passion I picked up my camera and pulled him by the hand and we went downstairs and out to the patio where the others had gathered. Robert, Yvette's boyfriend, had arrived. Robert was tall like Yvette, and good-looking with curly hair. He was standing there by Yvette at the table as she set out the plates. Mother and Octavia were helping at the other end. After I introduced Robert and my father, Yvette and I brought out the various platters of eggs and bacon and muffins and, following us, Octavia brought out the jam tray and other miscellaneous condiments. Then Mother went in and got the pitcher of orange juice. Now Austin was in his natural place, at the head of the table. I sat down to his right, my usual place, and when I saw my father beginning to sit between Robert and Octavia, I said, "Oh, no you don't." And I patted the seat next to me. "You're sitting right here next to me." And everybody laughed and he came over and sat down beside me. Then I said, "Let's all hold hands." I took my father's hand and my husband's hand. We all held hands and closed our eyes. Then Austin said grace, a short, to-the-point prayer of gratitude. I glanced at Mother down the table and she was looking cheerier than before as she reached for the muffins and held them in front of Octavia, saying, "Just take one at a time, now. Don't let your eyes be bigger than your stomach." And I remembered her saying those same words to me when I was a child and I had to choke back resentment. One thing I dreaded was her influence on Octavia. I felt that in many ways she had given me an unnecessarily hard time, had often struck me in rage for minor things, and had nagged me constantly when I was growing up. I felt in myself a tendency to treat Octavia this way and I was on guard all the time against the tendency. I meant to break the cycle. All the more reason why I was leery of Mother's presence around Octavia. Anyway, this was a happy moment and I wasn't going to let anything spoil it. I had put the camera down at the end of the table. Just before we started to eat, I looked down the table and said, "Robert, do me a favor. Please take a picture of my father and me together here like this at the table?" And I could see everybody glancing at me, understanding my eagerness, and sympathizing with me. I was acting frantic, acting like I thought he was going to suddenly disappear and I'd never see him again. And the fear wasn't unfounded. So Robert, a sweetie, got the camera and stood up and went into a crouch and snapped the picture as I leaned closer to my father, my face cheek-to-cheek with his. Later, after brunch, we took more pictures. And before I knew it, it was eleven-thirty and I shouted, "Oh, Winona's going to *kill* me! We've got to get you back!" So I ran inside, grabbed my purse and car keys while my father shook hands with Austin and Mother and Robert and kissed my sister on the cheek. Octavia hopped in the back seat and we drove back down to Fifty-fifth and Indiana Avenue. Octavia waited in the car. And we walked into Mother Zoe's kitchen exactly at five minutes to twelve. Both Mother Zoe and Winona were dressed now and both were sitting at the kitchen table smoking cigarettes and drinking instant coffee. Giving me this severe look, her crazy look, the first thing Mother Zoe said to her son was "You have a nice time?" and he said, "Yes, very nice." And she wanted to know who else was there. And my heart stopped. I tell you, my heart literally stopped because I had forgotten her concern. I started to say something but couldn't. Then my father said, "Oh, just Ophelia's sister and her boyfriend." And the relief I felt was obvious, maybe too obvious. I'd been holding my breath, then I let it go. And it was then, for the first time, that I thought to ask my father how long he was planning to stay, and he said, "I'm leaving in the morning, Ophelia. Gotta get back. An important transaction coming up. I'm representing both the buyer and the seller this time and it's a very sensitive situation.

But I'm coming back when I can stay longer. Okay?" But all I heard was him saying he had to leave and it caused something in me to cave in and I couldn't hide my feelings. With all my might I tried not to start crying and shaking. Somehow I'd thought he would be around at least a week. At *least*. I sighed and said, "Can I take you to the airport?" But Winona answered for him, saying, "That's all right, Ophelia. I've already asked for the morning off so I can drive him out to O'Hare." And I said, "Oh, I see. Then I guess this is the last time I'll see you, at least for a while. Huh?" I could feel the tears coming up again and I didn't want Winona and Mother Zoe to see me cry again so I said, "Come out to the car with me and say goodbye to Octavia. Okay?" And he followed me back out the back door, down through the backyard, out the gate, to the curb where Octavia was sitting at the wheel pretending to drive. By now I was shaking all over and tears were running down my cheeks and I didn't give a damn who knew it. I was miserable. He squatted down by the car door and spoke softly to Octavia for a minute or so, then stood up and I grabbed him and hugged him. I know I was being dramatic, too melodramatic. But I couldn't help it. It was how I felt. I didn't know how to feel or be any other way. I held him like it was the last time I would ever see him. And, like I said, that was five years ago.

Snipers

The owls are impossible, priceless,
a hundred points at least. They live at night
and call from the dark like children.
Their heart-shaped faces, their moth-like silences—.
But the carrion crows are obvious.
They enter the pines with parts of their wings
still caught in sunlight. Four, then five
of them bitching, ragging the emptiness.
Something in the wind and they last
a moment, heavy but flawless. Followed
by the jays, just as painful and skillful.
Jay-jay kee-yeeer kee-yeeer, jay-jay kee-yeeer.
One boy the first week bagged six crows' heads,
endless mice and rat tails, bodies of birds
too small to cut, a possum, whole,
and plumages of squirrels . . .
He brought his gun to show and tell
its tunnel barrel, its abstract accuracy.
The gun said jays were too quick, too beautiful,
the owls, in their Indian headdress, invisible.
It said that only the crows wear crowns
and sit in the gunsights of the trees' silhouettes
dancing but not moving. Redwings, mockers,
and the oriole were songbirds by comparison.
Another boy, at fifty points apiece,
tried to pass off starlings' heads for crows',
diminutive, yellow-billed, and dull.
He was the fool. I fooled and aimed at the trees.
The idea was to kill them back to the first crow,
the ghost crow made out of cloud,
to alter their next future.
The idea was arithmetic and order.

I remember that future now, the sixty
or so subspecies of sparrow
and the dead black weight of the burlap
doubled and dragged. The schoolroom
stank and the floor was slick with sawdust,
the iron lung and the slaughterhouse
the other long field trips that year.
At the window the rain-black light of a storm.
He said he wanted to shoot their eyes out or blow them
into the wind—kingdom come, that was the phrase,
as if the crows could care, being spiritual or suicidal,
here in the afterlife of memory and unaccountable crows,
where we'll never kill them all, nor see an owl.

ADRIAN C. LOUIS

Buffalo Spirit Song

for Robert Gay, 1946–1993

Great God
of any particular mood.
Sometimes it is all
too bovinely obvious.
Driving home from the Indian college
I followed a car jammed full
of buffalo heads snaking
along the road to White Clay.

Belching smoke on a blistering day
the rusted heap of a car cruised,
exuding the miasma of red
men with holes in their souls
and not one thin dime
for a bottle of ease.
It is a picture I have recorded
a thousand times and more.
There is nothing new here
except an invisible change in philosophy.
I used to think that if real men
did exist, then they existed on the wires
of that eternal magnetism
between cock and cunt.
I now know that real men
do not exist and never have.
I speak as a member
of a herd of mammals
who can dance and cry words on paper.

Note to a Culture Vulture

Some years ago
in your infinite European boredom
you finally concluded
that maybe Indians *are* really
a noble race, yes, somewhat tragic
but definitely tied to the earth.
So, you decided to become one.
Why not? Who would care?
And who would know the difference?
Your cheekbones *were* a little high
and you *were* a little dark.
Besides, everyone has an Indian passed out
in the rotting branches of their family tree.

Days sneaked into years while feathers
took root in your brain
and burst through your skull
to air-dance dry.
With your beaded words
and researched knowledge you became
well-known as a *Native American* writer.
I envied your university job
and I used to say that you were just
another fucking white thief
stealing what little we have left
but I just bought your new book
and I liked it, a little.

Rhetorical Judea

Most of my life I courted simplicity
and tried to leash any wind-breaking plagues
of rhetoric that swirled in my brain.
I prayed for rational segues from word
to deed, pain to relief, and madness to sanity
with little success so sometimes words
surged like mad lemmings to my tongue
and I spoke from a lopsided ether.

Most of my life had been led without Jesus.
Young, I built a tower around him from bricks
of doubt cemented with white lies
but he busted out and is sneaking around.
We all change. The great cliché I used to run to
was "misspent youth." Quaint, but yes,
at nineteen I became an alley cat,
snarling and spitting on cheap wine,
dining in rescue mission soup lines,
and humping anything on two legs.
No golden coin of the realm
was used in my rutting.
My one-eyed divining rod literally
led me by the hand for two decades.
Now, I'm scared of dying,
and I feel compelled to confess to the world!
I'm addicted to television and the IRS
is on my ass, but I shun those
who don't shun excess.
My latest God's eye is this:
I've abandoned those
who seek wild abandon.

This year I have been praying to stop
my rhetoric from defiling wisdom and maybe

that's the reason why I won't get drunk
and chase women with Verdell
who can't get past thinking the white man
tossed us down this sewer and we can't get out.

I've tried to tell him that we've become addicted
to eating shit, that we like the rank taste and tune.
I've tried to tell him many things
but his full-blood ass just won't listen
and the Great Spirit...well, the Great Spirit
needs his ears dewaxed
and Jesus, Jesus Christ of rhetorical Judea,
now paging Jesus, now paging Jesus!

Stories a Man Keeps to Himself

*"...for it seemed to me that everybody ought to know about
it, but I was afraid to tell, because I knew that
nobody would believe me..."*
—from *Black Elk Speaks*

It's a strange night here in West Virginia, warm
for November, one last thunderstorm before winter
comes on. Rain rattles against metal
awning, as if Oglala drummers circled
my house. They pound hollow bones against skinned
logs. Perhaps long thighbones of Wasichu
killed last summer, or buffalo slaughtered long ago
after a boy's first hunt.

        This is the way I think these days.
When I read what Black Elk dreams, and what he remembers,
I know something creeps into me that keeps me awake at night
and that I take with me when I sleep. How a Sioux man
falls in love with a woman and follows her even though
she will not talk to him. He hides in the bush near
the river where she bathes or washes clothes. He waits
for hours just so he can be alone with her and talk about love.
He offers a dozen ponies he does not have, or a hundred,
because he knows he will borrow or steal them if he has to,
just so he can love her forever.

        I know I have no right
to that man's life, and that Black Elk did not live
or die so that I might make this poem. I am Wasichu, I live
in a box. My music is not his music, I have no fire, and I
could not kill a man even if I hated him. I'd be the first
to die in a fight, or hunting buffalo for three days in deep snow.

But there are stories I can't get rid of, so many lives
crowded inside me, not in my head
so much, but in my chest, where the Greeks found
the soul—*pneuma,* they called it; "pneumonia" what we call
the sickness that steals our breath—and it is a kind of sickness
that Black Elk felt when he lay in fever for twelve days
and journeyed with his grandfathers, and that I feel
in the wing bones of my hips the day after
I make love to the woman I'd give
anything to have besides me now. A hundred
nimble ponies.

But tonight there's just this strange rain
beating on my roof. The only other sound is moths
hurling their bodies against the porch light, as if mad
spirits possessed them, crazy for paradise.

The Night Nurse

Don't doubt there's a future. Rushing toward you.

It was flat pavement, a busy pedestrian mall between downtown streets where she was walking in the tattered sunshine of a moist April morning when without warning the sidewalk tilted to her left, and a sharp pain like a wasp's stinging attacked the calf of her left leg. Wide-eyed and astonished, too surprised at this time to be frightened, she did not scream. She was not the kind of person to scream, especially in a public place.

She fell heavily on her side. Her glasses went flying, her handsome leather handbag dropped from her fingers, the side of her face struck concrete. Her immediate thought was *I've been shot.* The pain was so sudden and so absolute.

Strangers hurried to help. They seemed, to the stricken woman, to be materializing out of the air, with remarkable swiftness and kindness. Afterward she would count herself lucky that she was a well-dressed, well-groomed Caucasian woman stricken in this particular pedestrian mall with its Bonwit's, its Waldenbooks, its gourmet food store and pricey boutiques, and not elsewhere on the fringes of downtown. She was lucky that her handbag wasn't taken from her in the confusion of her fall and that strangers perceived her as one of their kind and not someone diseased, homeless, threatening.

She would remember little of her collapse afterward except its suddenness. And the terrible helplessness of her body fallen to the pavement. An ambulance arrived, its deafening siren translating to her confused brain as a lurid neon-red color. White-clad youngish medics examined her, lifted her onto a stretcher. As in a dream she was being borne aloft. A crowd of curious, snatching eyes parted for her. Alive? Dead? Dying? No one, least of all the stricken woman, seemed to know.

And in the speeding ambulance delirious with pain and mounting terror, an incandescent bulb of pain in her left leg just below the knee but still she did not scream biting her lips to keep from screaming and thinking even at this time *I am behaving well, look how calm and civilized.* Then she was being carried into a room glaring with laser-lights, again the quick purposeful hands of strangers probed her, her blood pressure was taken and blood extracted from her limp arm and her voice faltered trying to explain to someone she could not see what had happened to her, the pain in her leg more terrible than any pain she'd known, and a tightness in her chest and shortness of breath but she did not break down sobbing nor did she ask *Am I dying? Will I die?* nor did she beg *Save me!* Her name was Grace Burkhardt and she was forty-four years old and she was a woman accustomed, as the chief administrator of a state arts council, to exercising authority but she seemed to remember none of these external facts as if they applied not to her but to another person and that person a stranger to her. She wanted to explain *I am in good health, I can't believe this has happened to me* as if to repudiate responsibility but she was fainting and could not speak. They would check her identification, they would contact her nearest-of-kin, they would rush her into surgery and all this would be done apart from her volition and so there was a perverse comfort in that—in knowing that, if she died, now, it would not be her fault.

Of course they saved her. Emergency surgery for a "massive" blood clot in her leg which, had it broken free and been carried to her heart, would have resulted in a pulmonary embolism. Grace Burkhardt, dead at the age of forty-four never regaining consciousness even to realize the future had been condensed into the present tense and all was over.

By degrees she woke moaning in the post-op room not knowing where she was but knowing that this was a place strange and frightening to her. And so cold!—she was shivering, her teeth chattering. She experienced a sensation of utter sick helplessness as if she were paralyzed. She could not recall the surgery, or having collapsed. She could not recall if she had been saved from death or was even now being prepared for death. Her vision was blurred as if she were underwater. A face floated near, a stranger's face that was at the same time familiar as a lost sister's.

Help me! she begged the face. *I'm so cold, I'm so frightened!*

The face was a woman's. The features were indistinct but the skin was strangely flushed and shiny, like something not quite fully hatched. There was a smile, thin-lipped and tentative. No-color eyes. *Don't leave me, help! I'm so frightened!* Grace Burkhardt begged as like a large bubble playful and elusive the face rose, lifted lighter than air to disappear through the invisible ceiling.

Her nearest-of-kin was a married, older sister who drove forty miles from Rochester to be with her, staying through much of the day. As news of her "emergency surgery" spread among friends, acquaintances, colleagues at the arts council, there were telephone calls and the first of the floral deliveries. The public self, the self that was Grace Burkhardt, and not this woman in a hospital bed hooked to an IV gurney, her left leg raised and immobile swathed in bandages, struggled to emerge. You could not have guessed that Grace Burkhardt had survived a life-threatening collapse for, on the phone, she was wry, ironic, slightly embarrassed, determined to minimalize her condition. Her eyes were ringed with fatigue, her skin waxy-white, yet her voice maintained its usual timbre, or almost. Nothing meant more to her than to take back the control she'd lost back there in the pedestrian mall, to tell her story as if it were her own. For it was her own. *You wouldn't believe it! So suddenly. Yes, this morning. Yes, downtown. By ambulance. No, no warning. Yes, vascular surgery. A Dr. Rodman, do you know him? Yes, I'm lucky. I know. If it had to happen at all.*

Her sister finally took the telephone from her. She was protesting but too weak to prevail. Her head rang like the interior of a giant seashell. The pain in her leg was a balloon floating at a little distance from her—recognizable as her own, yet not *her. My name is Grace Burkhardt, my name is Grace Burkhardt* believing that this fact would save her. If anything would save her.

A powerful anti-coagulant drug was dripping into her veins to forestall more blood clots—that would save her.

The telephone messages. Daffodils, hyacinth, narcissus from the arts council staff, a potted pink azalea from a woman friend, another potted azalea so vividly crimson she could not look directly at it—these would save her. And the vascular surgeon who'd operated on her and saved her life, who came by the room to speak with her and with her sister. And her own doctor, an internist associated with the hospital who also dropped by on his rounds. And medical insurance forms, with which her sister helped her, and which, in a frail spidery hand, she signed. *You see? I'm fine, my mind hasn't been affected at all.*

And abruptly then, the day ended. This day that stretched dreamlike behind Grace Burkhardt as if to the very horizon to a region she could not see, nor even recall. It was evening, and she was alone. A nurse came to examine her and to give her a barbituate, a nurse's aide, a young cocoa-skinned woman, came to take away her bedpan discreetly covered with an aluminum lid, the light in her room was switched off. She called her sister's name not seeming to recall her sister's actual departure. Now alone, with no witness to admire her bravery, she tasted panic. Her left leg was swollen and stiff encased in bandages and elevated above the bed to reduce the condition the surgeon called "thrombophlebitis" which was the way, she understood, that death would enter her. The crepey-soft interior of her right elbow stung with a mysterious IV fluid dripping into a vein. Death would come as a lethal blood clot or death would come as a sudden massive hemorrhage that was the result of anti-coagulant medication. Though the stricken woman had not prayed in more than thirty years her parched lips moved silently *Help me through the night. Help me through the night.*

She felt a moment's rage at the injustice—that she, a good person, a woman known for her intelligence and her graciousness and her dependability in all things, a woman so widely liked, yes and respected, should be in this position, a life-threatening position. And trapped.

Help me through the night dear God, oh please!

As mercifully the contours of the room melted, the floor sank into darkness as into a pit, the powerful sleeping pill took her.

But then she woke, agitated and open-eyed as if she hadn't slept at all.

As if someone had called her name—"Grace Burkhardt."

There was a pinching sensation in her bladder, an urgent need to urinate. And such cold, why was the room so cold?—she woke shivering beneath a freezing sheet, a single-ply flannel blanket. The hospital by night was perceptibly cooler than by day. A ventilator rumbled, drafts of cold air passed over her. She'd been dreaming strangely and hadn't there been birds' wings flapping overhead stirring the air against her face...

"Grace Burkhardt."

The door had opened, now the door was closed. Someone had been in the room?—Grace tried to sit up, frightened, but was nearly immobilized. A sudden movement awakened pain, her heart's panicked throbbing that was pain, a sharp stinging in her right arm. Her eyes, mildly myopic, dulled with medication, moved blinking in the dark, this was an unfamiliar dark, she understood it was not her bedroom in her home nor any bedroom in her memory. The smell of disinfectant, the ventilator smell. The compression of space that was the size of a cell. She stared at the door a few yards away seeing a rim of light beneath it. For some moments she tried to remember where she was, and why such discomfort and pain, her leg elevated and held fast, her heartbeat so accelerated. As if pulling out of the dark a tangled dream of such complexity, the very effort was exhausting. She heard herself moan but the sound seemed to come from another part of the room. It was self-pity, it was terror and animal pain, it was not *her. I almost died, I'm in the hospital. I'm alone.* Struggling to sit up, to raise her head which swayed dangerously heavy on her shoulders, in a sudden mad terror of choking on her own tears and saliva and the mucus rapidly forming in her sinuses.

She fumbled to switch on her bedside light. Her sister had bought a traveler's digital clock in the gift shop downstairs—it was 2:55 a.m. She would never get through the night.

Yet she tried to calm herself. She was a patient in an excellent suburban hospital, she could not possibly be in danger of dying. *Help me! Help me I'm alone* but she rang the bedside buzzer because she desperately needed a bedpan. The barbituate had apparently knocked her out so completely, at 8:30 p.m., she hadn't wakened until the need to urinate was painful. And she needed an extra blanket. She rang the buzzer as she'd been instructed earlier to ring it and waited and there was no reply over the intercom so she rang it again and still there was no reply and so she counted twenty before ringing it again *Where are you? Isn't anyone there? Please help me* and this time a voice, a female voice, sounded over the intercom asking curtly what did she want and she explained her needs as clearly and politely as possible and the voice mumbled what sounded like *Yes ma'am* and was gone.

And now she waited. Waited and waited. It was three a.m., it was 3:10 a.m., it was 3:16 a.m. She could not get a comfortable position in the bed, her bladder so stricken, her leg at such an angle. Each second was agony. She tried to contract her lower body, her loins, as, as a small child, she'd tried to hold in the warm pee by pressing her thighs as tightly together as possible and not moving, hardly breathing. If she had an accident, urinating in the bed!—if that happened! All her life's history, all the striving of her very soul—to come to *that*. She felt a helpless child-anxiety she hadn't recalled for nearly forty years. The child-anxiety deep in the body of the adult. Remembering the agony of being trapped in some place (in the car, her father driving and unwilling to stop; in school assembly where she would have had to push her way out over the legs of her classmates enduring their jeering attention and the annoyance of her teacher) unable to get to a bathroom. The shame of it. The helplessness.

She rang the buzzer another, protracted time. Just as, thank God, the door was pushed open, and a nurse entered carrying a bedpan.

The night nurse, so short as to seem almost dwarfish. Hardly five feet tall. But round-bodied, with a moon face, peculiar flushed skin that was smooth and shiny as scar tissue; small close-set damp eyes; a thin pursed mouth. At a first glance the nurse might appear young but closer up she was obviously middle-aged, her eyes bracketed by fine white creases. "Here, lift up, like this, come *on*—" she issued instructions to the patient not so much coldly as mechanically, shoving the enamel bedpan beneath her buttocks, pulling down but not replacing the covers. Her manner was brisk and on the edge of impatience as if she and the patient had gone through this routine many times already and there was no need for coyness.

Grace's teeth were chattering with cold. She whispered, flinching under the nurse's unsmiling stare, "Thank you—very much." She could not help herself but began urinating immediately, as soon as the receptacle was in place, while the nurse was still in the room, though on her way out, turning away from Grace as if in disgust. No further words, no questioning of the patient if she needed anything else, no backwards glance. But Grace Burkhardt trapped in the bed was so grateful for this awkward receptacle, this adult-size potty, in which to empty her bursting bladder, she scarcely noticed the nurse's rudeness. If it was rudeness.

Her eyes smarted with the tears of gratitude and humility. Even the pain in her leg seemed to subside. The panicky numbness in her brain. But how long she urinated, in a gush of scalding liquid, then a thinning stream, ceasing and beginning again, she did not know. Minutes? Actual minutes? Looking at the clock finally, when the last of the urine dripped from her, she saw it was 3:38 a.m.

Outside the room's single window it was night. Yet not true night for the room, being lighted now, was reflected in the glass; not as in a mirror but dimly, shapes without substance or color.

I could die here in this room. Others have died here.

She'd had a lover once who had been terrified of hospitals. An intelligent man, a reasonable man, yet, on the subject of hospitals, adamantly irrational. Hospitals are seething with germs, hospitals are where you die. Hospitals are where you have to entrust strangers with your life and you pay for the privilege.

A lover, and not a husband. So many years later, Grace could not be clearly remember which of them had loved more deeply, which had been more hurt.

Now they lived a thousand miles apart, and kept in touch by telephone, a few times a year. Thank God they no longer had any mutual friends who might tell him of her collapse, her emergency surgery. *Massive blood clot. Risk of embolism.* He knew her as a healthy, independent woman. Not the kind of woman you feel sorry for.

Now Grace was finished with the bedpan, and the sharp smell of urine pinched her nostrils, she waited for the night nurse, or an attendant, to come take it away. Surely they knew, at the nurses' station?—she hesitated to ring the buzzer again.

So she waited. It was 3:40 a.m., it was 3:50 a.m. Finally, shyly, she rang the buzzer. There was no reply over the intercom.

Maybe the night nurse was making rounds. Giving medication, checking patients. Maybe, routinely, she would be back in a few minutes. Maybe she would bring an extra blanket.

At four a.m. Grace rang the buzzer again. There was a sound of static or shrill voices, then silence. "Hello? Hello—" her voice was plaintive, faltering.

Could die here in this room. Others have died here.

The enamel bedpan was pressing into the soft flesh of her buttocks. The elevation of her leg, and its stiffness, made the pressure more intense.

And how cold the room was—freezing. A continual draft from the window and another, smelling of something dank, metallic, unclean, from the air vent overhead.

In desperation she wondered if she could remove the damned bedpan herself. But set it where? On the bedside table, only a few inches away? And what if she spilled it, as certainly she would?—it was impossible to lift herself and to remove the bedpan at the same time. And now her leg, the entire left side of her body, was throbbing with pain.

She rang the buzzer again, trying not to panic. Though the intercom was dead she begged for help—"Please, can you come? I need medication, I'm in pain. I need a blanket—"

If the night nurse withheld the painkiller from her, what would she do?

Don't be absurd. Why would a complete stranger want to hurt you resolved not to give in to panic though she was trapped in this cell of a room in this bed at the mercy of the nursing staff. Whom she knew it would be a mistake to antagonize, especially so early in her hospitalization—Dr. Rodman had told her she might have to be here a week or more, thrombophlebitis is a serious condition. And her sister, meaning well, had told her alarming tales of negligent and even hostile nurses and attendants at big-city hospitals as a way of assuring Grace that here, by contrast, in this suburban hospital, she would receive better treatment.

At night, the hospital seemed very different than it did by day. It was closed to visitors until 8:30 a.m. In a panicked fantasy, Grace imagined a fire, at once she could smell smoke, and she, here, trapped, crippled with pain, paralyzed. If she wrenched her leg free, would its wound be torn open?—would she begin to bleed? She shuddered, whimpering to herself. Trapped! Trapped on a bedpan! It was ludicrous, it was laughable! Her own urine sloshing beneath her, threatening to spill and soak the bed.

She thought she heard the door being opened, the doorknob turning—but no. If there were footsteps out in the corridor they were gone now.

Strange how the hospital was not much quieter at night. A different and more mysterious kind of sound prevailed—a ceaseless churning like a motor turning over, never quite starting; a deeper throbbing like a jazz downbeat, but arhythmic, irregular. Beyond the vibrating of the ventilator there were distant voices. Pleading, crying. *Help me. Help. Me. Help me.* The voices overlapped, drowning one another out.

When she stopped breathing to listen more closely, the voices faded.

Grace did not want to think whose voices these were.

It seemed to her that she could feel tiny blood clots forming in her afflicted leg, like rain at the point at which it turns to sleet. If a single one of these clots broke free into her bloodstream it would be carried to her heart, to her pulmonary artery, and kill her.

What it is, what finality—to fall to the ground, on dirty pavement, at the feet of strangers. Grace Burkhardt now knew.

She pressed the buzzer another time. The intercom remained dead.

"Help me! Where are you!"

She was agitated, on the brink of hysteria and yet, somehow, she was falling asleep. The room began to shift and lose its contours; the light rapidly fading as if sucked down a drain. The bedpan filled with cooling piss, *her* piss, began to melt, too, its hard enamel warmed by her body. She'd drawn the inadequate covers up to her chin and her eyes were starkly open waiting for the night nurse to return and suddenly she saw—was it possible?—

the night nurse *was* back, had been back for some time, evidently?—standing motionless, watching her, just inside the door.

"Grace Burkhardt."

The nurse enunciated these syllables in a flat, nasal, ironic
voice.

"Grace Burkhardt."

Grace whispered, frightened, "Yes? Do you know me?"

It was as if she'd never heard her own name before. Never heard
its strangeness before.

The nurse's thin lips stretched in a smile. Her small close-set
eyes shone with the opacity of glass marbles. "Do you know *me*,
Grace Burkhardt?"

Grace stared. Quick as a thread pulled through the eye of a needle and out again she *knew*—knew the woman, or knew the girl
the woman had been; but she remembered no name; and did not
remember that face. She heard herself saying, quickly, "No. I've
never been in this hospital before. I've never—" Her voice trailed
off weakly.

There was an awkward pause. The nurse continued to stand
motionless, arms folded tight across her breasts. Her peculiar
shiny-smooth skin that looked like scar tissue, or like something
incompletely hatched, was the color of spoiled cantaloupe. Her
lips were bemused, childish in derision. "You wouldn't remember, Grace Burkhardt. No, not *you*."

The stricken woman lay trapped in bed. Her stiff throbbing leg,
her arm hooked to an IV apparatus. *She's mad, she's come to injure
me* though smiling at the nurse, trying to smile. As if this was an
ordinary exchange. Or might become so, if she smiled the right
way, if she spoke the right words. "I—can't see very well. My
glasses—my eyes— *Do* I know you?"

The nurse made a derisive laughing sound though her eyes
showed no mirth. She jerked her chin at the bed—"You're finished there, eh? Grace Burkhardt? So you want *me* to take it
away?"

Quickly, apologetically, Grace said, "If you would, please—"

"Registered nurses aren't required to touch bedpans."

"Then—an attendant? Could you call one?"

The nurse shook her head slowly. Bemused, disgusted. Still she stood without moving, arms folded across her breasts. In that face, in those eyes, Grace saw—who? It had been years. Half her lifetime. *No! No I don't know you!* She whispered, pleading, "Please, I'm helpless. I need medication, I'm in pain. And this bedpan—"

"*You're* helpless. *You* need help. So what? 'Grace Burkhardt.'"

"Why do you keep saying my name? Do you know me?"

"Why don't you say *my* name? Don't you know *me*?"

Grace stared, and swallowed hard. *I am a good person, I am well-liked, respected.* Recalling how through the years of her career, in her several administrative positions at Wells College, and at the State University at Buffalo, and more recently on the New York State Council of the Arts, she'd been praised for her industry, her fair-mindedness, her diplomacy; her intelligence, her warmth, her inconspicuous competency. Hadn't she overheard, to her embarrassment, just the other day, two young women staff members at the arts council speaking of Grace Burkhardt warmly, comparing her favorably to her male predecessor. *I am an adult now, I am a professional woman, I am no one you know.* Grace heard herself saying in a voice of forced surprise, with a forced smile, "Harriet—? Is it—Zimmer?"

The nurse said curtly, "*Zink.* Harriet *Zink.*"

"Of course. Harriet *Zink.*"

Grace should have exclaimed what a coincidence, after so many years, twenty-five? twenty-six? so you became a nurse after all, you didn't give up, how wonderful, Harriet, I'm happy for you— remembering vaguely that Harriet Zink, one of her roommates for part of her freshman year at the State University at Albany had been enrolled in nursing school. But when she drew breath to speak a wave of nausea swept over her. She whispered, "—Please, I need help. My leg—the pain. And the bedpan—"

As if aroused by the word *pain*, the night nurse became more animated. She came closer to Grace, peering at her curiously, almost hungrily. Grace had not given Harriet Zink a thought, or hardly a thought, in twenty-six years, and now—what an irony! The mere face of Harriet Zink, with that childish moon face, now middle-aged—how repulsive! Grace recalled her ex-roommate's prominent front teeth, the peculiar blush of her skin, her unnerving manner that was both groveling and insolent—oh, unmistakable.

They'd lived on the fourth, top floor of Ailey Hall, one of the older residences south of campus near the university hospital. Entering freshman, class of 1967. They were of the same generation glancing at the other's third finger, left hand, to see if there was a wedding band. Neither wore one.

Harriet Zink was asking in a bright, mock-earnest voice, "How is Jilly Herman?" and Grace Burkhardt had to stop to think, "—Jilly Herman?" and Harriet Zink said impatiently, "Grace Burkhardt's roomie Jilly Herman—how is *she?*" Grace stared at her, perplexed. *I am dreaming this, am I dreaming this* trying not to show the fear she felt as Harriet Zink went on derisively, "The one with the cute blond curls, Jilly Herman," gesturing at her own steely-gray hair with exaggerated wriggly fingers, "—the one with the cute *ass.*"

Grace said, in a faltering voice, "—I haven't seen or heard from Jill Herman in twenty years." Though this was true it sounded weak, like a lie.

Harriet Zink said suspiciously, "You haven't? You expect me to believe that?" When Grace began to protest she cut her off with childish vehemence, "Oh no! I don't believe that! Gracie Burkhardt and Jilly Herman were *best friends.* I bet you still *are.*"

These words were mocking, singsong. Grace tried to maintain her smile which was strained and ghastly against her bared teeth. She explained that, after freshman year, she and Jill went their separate ways, speaking earnestly as if this exchange in the middle of the night in such circumstances was not at all extraordinary but normal, and no occasion for alarm. But Harriet Zink interrupted, "And what about Linda Mecky, and Sandy McGuire, and Dolly Slosson," spitting out these names Grace scarcely recalled, and had hardly given a thought to since graduation, "—Barbara West, Sue Ferguson—" the names of freshman girls who'd roomed on the fourth floor of the old sandstone residence hall in the fall of 1963.

There had been six rooms on the floor, all doubles except for the largest which was a triple to which Grace Burkhardt and Jill Herman and Harriet Zink were assigned. But Harriet Zink didn't arrive on campus until October, twelve days late; there'd been an "emergency crisis" in her family. (The residence advisor hinted that Harriet's mother had died, and there'd been other trouble besides. She warned the girls not to bring up the subject unless Harriet initiated it herself—which she was never to do.) By the time the mysterious Harriet Zink arrived at Ailey Hall, friendships and alliances had been formed among the fourth-floor girls in that quick, desperate way in which such relationships are formed in new, disorienting surroundings. There had not seemed space enough for another girl. There had not seemed any need for another girl. And there was the problem, too, of Harriet Zink.

I tried to be nice to you. I did what I could. How am I to blame.

Harriet Zink was demanding to know what of these other girls, and Grace Burkhardt was trying to explain she really knew nothing of them, she wasn't in contact with any of them, but Harriet Zink seemed not to believe her, and angry that she should be lying. Grace tried to explain that most of them had only been friends during freshman year and that had been a kind of accident, stuck away on the top floor of Ailey Hall so far from the center of campus life, she tried to evoke the shabby comedy of Ailey Hall with its falling plaster and its leaky windows and its cockroaches, but Harriet Zink kept interrupting, pursuing her own line of inquiry. "Do you remember what you did to me? You, and your friends?" Her face was heated and her small eyes brightly moist. There were half-moons of perspiration beneath the arms of her snug-fitting white nylon uniform and Grace remembered across the abyss of twenty-six years a snug-fitting clumsily homemade red plaid jumper of Harriet Zink's whose underarms were permanently stained. "Don't say you don't remember, Grace Burkhardt!"

Grace frowned, innocently perplexed. She was miserable in her bed, her leg pounding in pain, her head pounding, and, dear God, the sharp smell of urine penetrating the covers, had she spilled some of the urine into the bed, she bit her lip to keep from sobbing *I must not let her see I'm afraid of her, I must stay calm* shaking her head saying, "No, please, Harriet, I don't—" which brought the angry little woman closer to the bed, how like a dwarf she was, so short, and stouter now that she'd been at the age of eighteen, her face rounder, puffier, and that mouth made you think of a slug, always moving, working. Harriet Zink said in a tone of near-dignity, "*I* remember. *I* still dream about it sometimes."

Grace said softly, "Harriet, I'm sorry."

"Huh! How can you be sorry, if you don't remember?"

"Please, I'm in pain. If you could help me—"

"*I* was in pain. You didn't help *me*."

"—I need medication. Painkiller. Please. And this bedpan—please could you take it away—"

"I told you: registered nurses aren't required to take away bedpans. That's not our job."

You never took showers or baths. You wore your clothes until they were filthy. You smelled. You stank. You cried yourself to sleep every night. How am I to blame! Grace knew, yet didn't know: couldn't quite remember. It was so long ago, it was like a bad dream, not her own dream but another's. What exactly had happened between the time Harriet Zink, who like Grace Burkhardt was from a farming family in the central part of the state, and the weekend before Thanksgiving when she moved out of Ailey Hall, dropped out of nursing school. Disappeared. *I tried to be nice to you. I did what I could. How am I to blame!*

In a lowered, quavering voice Harriet Zink was saying, "You and Jill Herman, you wouldn't talk to me. I'd be there in the room and you'd send each other signals. Look right through me. Like I was dirt. If I came into the lounge you'd all stop talking and make like there was a bad smell. If I came into the cafeteria where you were all sitting you'd look away and freeze me out. You knew about my mother and how I cried at night and that was funny to you wasn't it. Everything about me was funny to you wasn't it. I was late starting classes and behind on all my work and you could see how scared I was, I couldn't sleep and I couldn't keep food down and all of you knew it, all twelve of you, but it was just a joke to you wasn't it—that I wanted to die."

Grace Burkhardt could not believe what she was hearing. She said, weakly, "Not me, Harriet. Not me. I tried—"

"Oh sure! You'd say to them sometimes, 'Let her alone.' Once in the downstairs lounge when they were laughing together you said to them, 'That's enough, it isn't funny, let her alone.' But you wouldn't say my name. You wouldn't ever say my name. It was like I was *it* to you. You wouldn't look at me even when we were alone together and if I talked to you, you'd just mumble something back and walk away. I could see in your face you felt sorry for me, sure, you pitied me like a leper, you thought you were so much better than me, you, 'Grace Burkhardt'! You tried to stop them from the worst of what they did but you didn't try hard *enough*."

"Harriet, I'm sorry. We were so young, then—so ignorant."

"You weren't ignorant. *You* were a scholarship student."

"We didn't mean to be cruel—"

"Yes you did! You meant to be cruel," Harriet Zink said, with angry satisfaction. "It made you happy, all of you, to be cruel."

"Harriet, no—"

Harriet Zink continued speaking in her low, accusing voice, her face now brightly flushed, recounting incidents Grace Burkhardt had long since forgotten, if indeed she'd ever known. She tried to remember how long pathetic Harriet Zink had actually roomed with her and Jill Herman before moving downstairs to a single room near the resident advisor's suite—that room kept in readiness for just such an emergency. *Yes, it's so. It made us happy. Our cruelty. Our loathing for the true freak among us.* After Harriet Zink dropped out of school, having failed more of her midterms, the girls of the fourth floor, including several nursing students to whom she'd been a particular embarrassment, had not missed her. Or, if they missed her, they did not dwell upon her absence. They did not consider its significance. It had nothing to do with them, did it?—*they* were normal, *they* were adjusting to college life. After Harriet Zink moved out of their room Grace and Jill cleaned it as they'd never cleaned it before, exhilarated, singing along with the Kingston Trio whose hit record Jill played repeatedly on her turntable, airing out the room, windows open to a bright dry autumn day, a breeze lifting papers on their desks. Gaily they vacuumed, they scrubbed. Their door was wide open to welcome their friends. *Sad to say, I'm on my way, won't be back for many a day* but their lifted voices, their shining eyes, were anything but sad. The third desk, in the corner, was bare. The third bed, beneath the tilt of the eave, was bare. Later, Grace would cover the bed with a beautiful afghan quilt knitted by her grandmother. The third desk was used by both girls. They were particularly grateful for the extra closet space.

Now Harriet Zink, middle-aged, squat body in her nurse's uniform solid as a little barrel, was leaning over Grace Burkhardt in her bed, saying, in disgust, " 'Grace Burkhardt'—you were the evil one among them because you were the one who *knew*. I could see it in your face. And right now! You knew, but you wouldn't help me, you wouldn't be my friend."

Grace said stammering, "Harriet, I'm—I didn't—" her eyes brimming with tears of shame, "—forgive me!" She was so frightened she'd leaned away from the angry woman and caused the IV needle to pop out of her vein.

There was a pause. Harriet Zink stared at Grace, leaning so close over her that Grace could see specks of hazel in the iris of her eyes; a glimmer of gold fillings in her mouth. Harriet was breathing harshly, like an overweight woman who has climbed a stairs too quickly. Yet her expression shifted suddenly, turned unexpectedly thoughtful. She said, with the air of one making a discovery, "Yes, I can forgive you, Grace Burkhardt. I'm a Christian woman. In my heart I'm empowered to forgive." She nodded gravely, as if, not knowing until this instant what she'd intended, what she would do, she was taking pleasure in it. "When I saw you here, Grace Burkhardt, and I thought, 'Am I strong enough to forgive that woman? Even with Jesus' help, am I strong enough?' I didn't know. But now I know. I *am* strong enough, I *can* forgive." She spoke with such sudden pride, it was as if sunshine flooded the room.

In this way, as a terrified Grace Burkhardt would not have anticipated, the siege ended.

For a long time after the night nurse left the room Grace lay unmoving too shocked to think even *How am I to blame! I tried, I did try* incredulous thinking *Evil—me? Of all people—me? The woman is a religious maniac.* She was too agitated to sleep yet somehow must have slept if only briefly and then waking opening her eyes wide and amazed that it was still night? still night? when in her dream she'd been staring into the sun as if in penance and her eyes were seared and aching.

She struggled to sit up. She could breathe better, sitting up. Her leg throbbed with pain, pain was like a wave that washed over her and through her leaving her exhausted but wakeful. The bedside lamp was still on. She'd thought the night nurse had turned it off. In the room's single window flat, ghostly reflections floated. She could not identify her own among them.

The night nurse, after her mad outburst, had treated Grace Burkhardt kindly. Or, if not kindly, with a brisk businesslike efficiency. She'd replaced the needle in Grace's bruised right arm, and saw that the IV fluid was dripping into her vein. She called an aide, a young black girl, to bring an extra blanket and to carry away, at last, the bedpan. But, as she explained, she could not give Grace any of the painkiller Oxycodone prescribed for her by Dr. Rodman because the next dosage was scheduled for seven a.m. By that time the day staff would be on duty and another nurse would take care of her. Thank you, Grace murmured, thank you so much, Harriet, humbled and grateful as a chastened child but the night nurse merely shrugged as if embarrassed and then she was gone.

It was only 4:54 a.m. The extra blanket seemed not to make much difference—Grace was still shivering, the room was still very cold. There was a smell of something close, damp, unclean like mold. There was a faint smell or urine. *Help me, help* but Grace had already rung the buzzer and she understood that she'd already been helped and that there was no more help. She decided to sit up sleepless through the remainder of this terrible night though believing, with the resigned half-humor of the damned, that it would never end. Never would it be dawn and never the miraculous hour of seven a.m. and a respite from pain. Thinking, *I am not that strong. I am not evil, but I am not that strong. In her place, I could not forgive.* When she looked at the little digital clock her sister had bought her she saw it was 4:56 a.m.

MARK JARMAN

Psalm: Let Us Think of God as a Lover

Let us think of God as a lover
　　Who never calls,
Whose pleasure in us is aroused
　　In unrepeatable ways,
God as body we cannot
　　Separate from desire,
Saying to us, "Your love
　　Is only physical."
Let us think of God as a bronze
　　With green skin
Or a plane that draws the eye close
　　To the texture of paint.
Let us think of God as life,
　　A bacillus or virus,
As death, an igneous rock
　　In a quartz garden.
Then, let us think of kissing
　　God with the kisses
Of our mouths, of lying with God,
　　As sea worms lie,
Snugly petrifying
　　In their coral shirts.
Let us think of ourselves
　　As part of God,
Neither alive nor dead,
　　But like Alpha, Omega,
Glyphs and hieroglyphs,
　　Numbers, data.

Unholy Sonnet

Amazing to believe that nothingness
Surrounds us with delight and lets us be
And that the meekness of nonentity,
Despite the friction of the world of sense,
Despite the leveling of violence,
Is all that matters. All the energy
We force into the match head and the city
Explodes inside a loving emptiness.

Not Dante's rings, not the Zen zero's mouth,
Out of which comes and into which light goes,
This God recedes from every metaphor,
Turns the hardest data into untruth,
And fills all blanks with blankness. This love shows
Itself in absence, which the stars adore.

KENNETH ROSEN

In Defense of the Fallen Clergy

For the priests accused of fondling altar boys,
Of using the orifice of communion and the other
Unnaturally, for heresies preached
Of whisper, nudge and dubious games,
Hand burning a thigh in dubious
Accident and secrecy,

The way elation cauterizes fear,
For the fevers of adrenalin wherein shame
Forges one an angel naked and invisible,
Loving and beloved in an ecstasy
Of occult fluttering, a fire
About to fall, yellow,

Crimson, tangerine. Now in the dark
Of night, the half-forgotten flame
Is a chimera, life again an ash
In the chaos of memory, a scandal
Detached from all holiness,
A spectacle. Oh everyone

Come see the priest who strayed
Who toyed with the altar boys'
Marbles and canes. And as for
The chosen, elevated and betrayed,
Twig, leaf, forest snail, and then
The unbelievable, a new

Confusion of church and pain,
Pride and quasi-certainties
Scarred by unseen difference,
And queerly afraid of difference,

Queerly bestirred, bewildered
As in made wild,

Who'd confront and complain,
Restore equilibrium by blending
Into mob America of the pious panic
And inertia, nothing, no pity, only
Anger and disdain. Shame is the basis
Of being. No one is clean.

Poetry Reading in Pisgah

So few attended the reading
Of my fabulous friend,
They moved us from the room with tinted windows
Overlooking the fern gardens and fountains
And rocks of moss, to a small bar
With black walls and red stools.

Beyond the swinging doors
Stuttered a mariachi trumpet,
And the imitation coyote yowls
Of hungry lovers. "The poet you're about to hear,"
I started, thinking how just last year
He'd had a heart attack playing frog

In the swamp, almost losing it
While gaining on a water lily, "writes poems
Of recovery from vast, nebulous losses,
And sad joy…" At that moment
A brace of waiters in ebony tuxedos
Burst toward the swinging doors

Bearing trays of shucked oysters,
Gray, quivering pyramids raised from deserts
Of lettuce, on each an oasis
Of cocktail sauce in a silver cup.
From the tequila people licking
Salt, sucking lemons, swallowing fire,

Rose a roar as when a bull is killed,
Stabbed in back of the horns. A door stuck open.
The Mexican trumpet sustained a crescendo,
The other room white as an oven's core.
I slid off my stool to restore quiet
And order, sanctum sanctorum,

But nothing could shut away
The cigarette smoke or light from that room,
Its stench of manure and perfume,
Its clatter of glasses, rudeness and laughter,
And the visiting poet put a hand on my shoulder
And began whispering lines

As if prayers, as if shifting
Our ashes and reading our clocks of sand,
Words for the gorgeous, violent uncertainties
Of the promised land which is always
A valley away, a view from the mountain,
The life and death of next door.

JAN SELVING

Offerings

Once mistaken for a man I began to dress like one.
Tall, broad-shouldered, hair cropped close,
I could wear seersuckers, double-breasted pinstripes,

disguised, free to go anywhere I pleased.
But I rarely spoke, and was the only woman
my rich, old neighbor would eat with.

After a day's shopping for mission oak in SoHo,
Brooklyn's Atlantic Avenue, we ate lunch
at Alfredo's while Tom watched the young waiters

dodge toward us, in and out of tables,
balancing plates of tortellini,
cold asparagus salad, his double chocolate cake.

He'd take a few bites then push the plate
to me, say, "Here, enjoy."
In the gym beneath the overpass

Saturdays, Tom and I sat ringside
as trucks ground above the barrio boys
dazed by smoke and lights,

listing against the ropes.
The bell would bring on Tom's Parkinson's—
foot scuttling, tapping cement floor,

the tremor quickly spreading to his leg,
hand clasped hard against his thigh.
I'd remember the first day he asked me in—

the small stone figure of a sleepy Etruscan
sat on a table near Tom's bed,
its smooth back burnished by his constant stroking,

as if this ancient citizen
might imbue Tom's body with rest.
In the last round the tremor passed

to the cloud of smoke above the crowd.
And I knew I'd have to make my own way home
as Tom rattled the bills he'd fold

into a fighter's satin pocket,
taking him like all the rest
to spar in his living room. The street's neon—

LINDEN LIQUORS, KNIGHTS OF COLUMBUS—
banding the walls, torsos flashing pink
then green as Tom lowered his gloves,

asking to be hit.
I did his laundry, cooked, arranged poppies
in a Roseville vase,

dusted his books, and the Etruscan,
a Tiffany shade's blue wisteria
while Tom sat and watched me work.

He gave me some beads,
cool green and mottled, Mayan.
"Everything's gray," he'd say. "Make it clean."

Isabel

After all there is still truth and delicacy.
    Shall I tell you of the fat man in the darkened theater,
or the Russian baritone and his waterbed? No, you want to hear

    about the scars, layered, scoring my wrists.
The man who still sends me his hair, pungent through the skin
    of the envelope, introduced me to the art

of humiliation, what he called the power of passivity.
    When he asked, I masturbated for his friends in the back
seat of his Cadillac as we cruised the skin shops

    on Eighth Avenue, then politely went down on them all.
Mornings sore, bruised, Kevin gave me breakfast in bed,
    and gifts—Roseville, Venetian jacquard, Schubert

Lieder, Outerbridge's carbroprint beauties. Blindfolded, hands
    cuffed behind my back, left in dark rooms like the menstrual
outcast, I'd begin to wander, the true recompense.

    When I was seven my father walked in to pee,
unaware I was bathing, and I was surprised yet remained hidden
    by mottled glass, safe within warm water till he left,

turning off the light behind him. It was a stranger darkness
    in Kevin's house—breath, a hand turning me over,
legs binding my waist as he placed his cock between my breasts.

    I grew numb from his weight, divided again
as once before when I was placed across a window, frame
    poised above my back like the blade of a guillotine.

While he fucked me I watched buildings spill hundreds—
   the street at rush hour, seeing miles—midtown to
the Brooklyn Bridge, an armory of lights, tankers docking

   in the harbor. Eleven stories above, omniscient—
no one looking to see the torso jutting from brick—
   the ship's muse and maiden figurehead.

Over All

Gored by the climacteric of his want
He stalls above me like an elephant.
—Robert Lowell

Stalls? I'd have wondered, *Has he died at last?*
Like Anthony's self-pity: *I am dying, Egypt, dying.*
Like Nelson Rockefeller undoing Happy on his hooker.
Like a stuck pig who hasn't seen the dripping knife,
Kemal Pasha's grunting, grunting, till his air gives out
And leaves me trapped and scared beneath him.
If he be rich and all our children blond...
If he be dead and I am found like this...
If, if, if...Whatever death this man fears most
It can't be this, caught under the obscene collapse
Of cooling flesh and blood and hair and bone.
One can feel the lost already beginning to rot.
Worse, one feels oneself going soft, then gone.
In the dresser mirror the small slice of him bursts
And glows and then grows quickly gray as ash
And one thinks, while waiting, Would it be better now
Or worse to have had that mirror hung above the bed?
So, when they called me from the hospital to say
He'd collapsed in a cab on his way to Logan
And was DOA in the ER at MGH, I thought:
That's O.K. That's great. Thank God the old fart
Didn't die on me, didn't die at six a.m.
When we were fucking, or in the shower, or at breakfast.
He didn't die on me! He rolled off. Dressed and left.
Still, I'll have to go downtown, I'll have to face
Confessing that I can identify his last remains.

In Mudville, In a Time of Plague

1.

For five days in October, Carlos died.
He could get himself up, up to the last.
I'm fine, he said, so I left him alone.
I went shopping, but then, when I got home,
He was dead, stiff, dressed in the three-piece suit
We'd bought at Penney's for his laying-out,
And lying curled like a cat in the tub.
I can't imagine what he'd been thinking.
Of course he shit and the suit was ruined.
The paras guessed it was a suicide,
Though one did say it was a goddamn shame—
She liked her lovers short, blond and handsome.
And mustachioed too, I'm glad I said,
Which shouldn't have bewildered her, but did.

2.

Indeed, as she always had in her life,
In her sudden death Emma surprised me.
Tell her my name is Emory, she said
When the emergency room clerk asked us
For proper identification.
*A life support system for a penis
Is all I am,* she told the scowling dyke.
That was Saturday before Thanksgiving.
By Monday she was dead. *His heart gave out,*
The doctor said. I shook my head. *Gave out?
Emma's?* I asked, as if he couldn't know:
Emory Chan. Chinese male. Thirty-two.
You have no rights in this matter, he said,
Turning a phrase in the heart of what hurt.

3.

Though we knew Morgan would die this winter,
We'd hoped for March, the last of it, leaden
And Lent, Christs and crocuses popping up
Purple and yellow all over the lawn.
God! That's garish! Morgan said at the last,
Meaning not the lawn, but his brother's shirt
Which was pale blue, a doctor's shirt seen through
The haze of drugs a doctor could provide.
Christmas is coming, Morgan's brother said.
Easter, Morgan said, and so they argued
For a while. *I'll be skinny in heaven,*
He said and his brother the doctor said,
Even skinnier.
                    I'll be a doctor,
Morgan said. *And straight, or even straighter.*

Another Comedy for Paolo and Francesca

Amor, ch'a nullo amato amar perdona,
mi prese del constui piacer sì forte,
che, come vedi, ancor non m'abbandona.
Amor condusse noi ad una morte.
— Dante

Is this hell, where neighbors will try to burn us out?
To clear the woods one doused a cat in gasoline
And let her run afire through the brush. August drought
And hatred does the trick. Heart of cinder, so mean
He has abandoned hope, he wants the world to moan
As he moans, to curse God, to breathe black air, to shake
In the sirocco empty hands like chimes of bone.
He calls down Jesus Christ. Come down! he cries, and make
Of earth a hell, this hell, here, now, in our despite.
Oh he loves Christ. For Christ he set the cat on fire,
He burned the rabbits—burned the doves rising like light
Out of the blazing pines—burns you for your desire.

Before fire interrupted my design
I had planned this homage to be a kind
Of garden—recompense of word and line
Whose ironies would, like an icy wind,
Disperse the flames whereby a jealous Christ
Punishes those lovers who dare to love.
I had hoped to quote Miss Marianne Moore
Who might have likened poetry to lust
When she said that she too disliked it, that poor
Second to what it is we really want.
Still, wasn't it poetry's little shove
That launched you from the frigid shore of can't?

She wants him to imagine this—
For a bed of flowers a field

Of ash. Inside each burned-out stump
A toad is waiting for her kiss
And inside him a soul Christ killed
For love and turned into a lump
Of coal to frighten children with
And inside it the light that failed
To become for the world a lamp.
She wants him to imagine this
So that what once had been filled
In her by his blood won't go limp.

What Dante used you for
Was no joke. You became
The lesson for all lovers:
Her beauty loosed the beast,
His honor tapped the whore.
We joke. We should not blame
Sex on the two fuckees.
We blame God who, all lovers
Must know, has rooted for
Our turpitude and shame
On which His own release
Depends. To hell with lovers

Is what God wills
Whenever He
Is so disposed
Or indisposed
By love. Our fires
Remind Him that
He gave us wills
To disobey
Even in hell
Commandments He
Designed to foil
What flesh desires.

FIELDING DAWSON

Under the Trees on the Hill

In the first week of the last month of the semester, a new young inmate came into the classroom, took a seat, and watched the teacher with sharp eyes. Soon he was involved with discussions—even wrote essays, original stuff, quick—zipped them off, so smart. Sharp, and charming, good-looking yet warm, yet an edge of violence. Soon embroiled in one of those classroom stews, where everybody speaks, yells, shouts, demands, implores, and teacher helpless, let it go, to witness and enjoy it: that afternoon loud and fervent on their neighborhoods and what who wanted to be most or—something, life's ambition not often clear in these debates, but of a sudden the new fellow's voice rose, and took command. So compelling teacher lost sense of the classroom, they were on a street corner, and he listened to this vivid tale of woe, told with verve, wit, and sparkle, in the most intense angry amusement:

"...you know that street that goes up a hill overlooking the river, near the academy?"

"Oh yes," teacher smiled, glancing at the other guys, seated in their desks, listening. Smiling. Eager.

"That's where I saw her car!" cried the youth. "You know, those trees along the sidewalk?"

Guys nodded.

"Yes." Teacher.

"Well, that's where I saw her car, parked. I knew her car."

"Okay."

Knowing something was coming, teacher looked at the guys, and grinned. They, too. Grinned.

"In front of his house," he said, bending a little, being slender, and small, as if to stretch himself longer, tense in anger and laughter, excited: eyes wide, pupils floating. Arms outstretched, fingers spread—"His house! The guy she was in love with! *He* was a cop! *I* wasn't, but she," he laughed, wild, "she *wanted* to be a cop, *she wanted to be a cop,* and—"

"Was parked in front of his house," teacher said, lips in a smile. Eyes not.

"*Yeah!* Because he was a cop! I saw her car. I know her car, and it was there, under the tree on the hill in front of the house where the *cop* lived!"

And a couple of weeks later, shook hands in that room, and said goodbye...the end of the last class before graduation ceremonies...sad, to say farewell. Teacher gave him his address saying keep in touch, sure! Sure! Knowing he never would and he was right, for the youth did not, but why, in truth, should he? Aside from the fact he had come into teacher's poetry class, and teacher had paid attention to him, what did that say, or do? Teacher was not the essential point. How the young man was responding to the car under the trees on the hill. That was the image, the poetic image, and the story without a plot told by an uneducated but talented, very intelligent, very angry, and perhaps too insecure youth, in a passing two or three classes, in the School Block, in a House of Detention for Men, in a big city somewhere, anywhere in America, a country where saying goodbye was tough, it hurt, but it was said more often that saying hello, and getting more and more the thing to do, the way things were going.

Teacher stood there, facing the empty chairs, in the empty classroom, looking out the dirty windows at the dry, gray weedy dirt between the cell blocks, under a low, even dirtier sky. He had to learn to let these guys go. He had to let them go where they would, wherever it was, because he was not the essential.

True.

But teacher was a resolute and caring man, and to let them go like that infuriated him—he knew he was not the essential, home and family were—but letting them go as if to the winds infuriated him because he remembered them all, thus they were memorable, and they *were* in the notes he kept, so they were in his way *of him.* This anger was in his eyes, in the set, determined expression of his lips, and across his face which caused certain prison guards to look twice at him, with murder in their longing eyes, because he hated them, and held them in contempt. Thus he wore his face in mask, so they looked at him and saw no one. A deception teaching in prisons had taught him, and he had learned, fast.

Bob Marley's Hair

The dreadlocks had all fallen off
from chemotherapy, and so
when Marley died in Switzerland
they flew the body in the hold

to Kingston, where he would lie
in state, or in the anti-state he'd
written all those hymns for, his face
ironed into repose and sweet,

or bland if sweet couldn't be done.
"Baldheads" is what Rasta call
white people. The body needed not
just hair, but the corkscrewed waterfall

in all the photographs, the coiled crown
he could fling that would spring back,
the curtain he could part or close,
his proud tatters. No wig could fake that.

So on the same flight Marley's
mother rode home with his dreadlocks.
Thirty-eight thousand feet they reached, and then
came down. On her lap, in a box.

President Reagan's Visit to New York, October 1984

Pomp churned through midtown like a combine,
razing a path to the Waldorf-Astoria.
At 34th and 10th a black man

drizzled a wan froth of soap and dirt
on my windshield and paused for me to pay
to get it squeegeed off. He just wanted,

he said, to make an honest living.
I gave a dollar and he gave thanks; we
knew the going rate, and then we went,

another poem might say, but a red light
like that can take forever to turn green,
our creamiest streets were cordoned off so

Pomp could clot them, and it seemed we'd spend
the rest of our lives that way: the Waldorf
bellboys (aged 23–59)

bantering, the black man with his back
to me, the light red and I stalled in rue,
the soot-slurred sky reflected by the smoked glass

windows of the limos as their cavalcade
neared the hotel, the shops gleaming with goods,
the impossible future, the tufted clouds.

Old Folsom Prison

Here's a romantic prison for you.
This could be Scotland: a crag and far below
the froth-marled river. Where is the stag,
the laird, where are the baying hounds?

Welcome instead to Hotel California.
Johnny Cash sang right there, in Graystone
Chapel, and from the blue, disconsolate
congregation he drew, like blood, whoops

and yelps enough to flood the place.
Rapists rose; and arsonists; and the man
who drew five lifetime sentences, without
parole, for vehicular homicide

(a mother and four kids), to be served
consecutively, rose also; as did
murderers enough to still all breath
in a small town; and armed robbers; and

sellers of dope to your children and mine,
and earlier, perhaps, to you and me.
In their blue work shirts and blue jeans
they swayed like wheat in a strong wind,

and when Cash sang that he'd shot
a man just to watch him die, their shouts
rose like so many crows you'd wonder where
there was room for air, if you were there.

Let's say you were. But for the grace of God
some other wretch would house your crow in his throat.
The way caps get flung at graduation,
crows thronged the air, and then they subsided.

New Folsom Prison

Heat sensors, cameras on automatic
pan, vast slabs of prefabricated wall
trucked in and joined on site like grandiose
dominos.... It took the state eight years

to plan to keep those men apart from you
and me and only sometimes from each other,
for even gang rapists and murderers
are social animals. One told me, "I belong."

He'd checked his math twelve years of nights
and he belonged. "They tell you how and where
this place was built?" he asked. They couldn't stop:
they told me six times. He knew that I knew,

but neither of us let on, for we had,
the ironist and the killer, begun
to talk, for neither of us was *they*.
"No," I said. "Think," he said. "They'd need," I tried,

"cheap labor." He smiled. "Where would they get it?"
And then there were two of me. One talked
to Robert, call and response. We knew how
the world worked, and on whose behalf. We knew

our grim parts. And the other of me saw
not *labor* but men, stark *camaradas*
brooding and cubicled like hens athwart
their hay- and shit-flecked eggs. Inmates elsewhere

in the California prison system
built New Folsom part by part, day by day,
and then lay down at night in their slim bunks
to dream of violence and manufacture.

Ohio

We were excited at the motel
when the B.B. King tour bus
pulled in but then my mother said
"Where did all these colored come from?"
She's eighty-five.
That's how it is in Ohio.

No it's not, that's how it is
in us, that's why thirty-five years ago
in my first year at Cornell
we elected the one black kid in my class
president though no one talked to him
and that's why last year when someone
left the note "DIE NIGGER" on Denise's desk
everybody said they couldn't *imagine* what
cretin would do a thing like that.

And I think that's why the great dream
of middle-class whites is to lie face-down
on a chaise by a pool in the sun,
left alone, not moving; why they dream
of a state as close to death as possible,
flat, bland, unending, like the Ohio
Turnpike and all the motels off it
and the food shops with their vats of grease
and their smells of burning fats and chemical
donuts glazed orange and blue and green
and the embalmed meats in infinite variety.
And no one murmurs: they buy and eat and eat.

On African-American Aesthetics

But since I've written just this one poem
About being black, having a black body,
I know that they have won—whoever they are.

And I know what it is like to wish for death.
Not the way people in poems do,
But the way successful suicides do—or did.

Little White Sister

Mama warned me, stay away from white girls. Once I didn't. So, thirty years too late I'm minding my mama. That's how it happened.

I saw her. Flurries that night and she's running, bare-legged, wearing almost nothing at all, and the snow's rising up in funnels, like ghosts, spinning across the street till they whip themselves against the bricks, and I'm thinking, Crazy white girl don't know enough to come in from the cold.

Crackhead most likely, not feeling the wind. I'd seen the abandoned car at the end of the block, ten days now, shooting gallery on wheels, going nowhere. One of them, I told myself, pissed at her boyfriend or so high she thinks her skin is burning off her. Most times crackheads don't know where they are. Like last week. Girl comes pounding on my door. White girl. Could've been the same one. Says she's looking for Lenny. Says she was here with him last night. And I say, *Lenny ain't here;* and she says, *Let me in.* I don't like arguing with a white girl in my hallway so I let her in. I say, *Look around.* She says, *Shit—this isn't even the right place.* She says, *What're you tryin' to pull here, buddy?* And I back away, I say, *Get out of here.* I say, *I don't want no trouble;* and she says, *Damn straight you don't want no trouble.* Then she's gone but I'm thinking: You can be in it that fast and it's nothing you did it's just something that happens.

See, I've already done my time. Walpole, nine years. And I'm not saying Rita's the only reason I went down, but I'm telling you, the time wouldn't have been so hard if not for the white girl.

Cold turkey in a cage and I know Rita's in a clinic, sipping methadone and orange juice. I'm on the floor, my whole body twisted, trying to strangle itself—bowels wrung like rags, squeezed dry, ribs clamped down on lungs so I can't breathe, my heart a fist, beating itself. And I think I'm screaming; I must be screaming, and my skin's on fire, but nobody comes, and nobody brings water, and I want to be dead and out of my skin.

Then I'm cold, shaking so hard I think my bones will break, and that's when the rabbitman slips in between the bars. The rabbitman says: *Once an axe flew off its handle, split an overseer's skull, cleaved it clean, and I saw how easily the body opens, how gladly gives itself up; I saw how the coil of a man's brains spill from his head—even as his mouth opens, even as he tries to speak. Then I saw a blue shadow of a man—people say he ran so fast he ran out of his own skin and they never found him, the rabbitman, but I tell you, they took my skin and I was still alive.* Then the rabbitman whispered: *I got news for you, little brother, I been talkin' to the man and he told me, it ain't time, yet, for this nigger to die.*

So no, I don't go chasing that girl in the street. I know she'll be cold fast, but I think, Not my business—let one of her friends find her.

See, since Rita, I don't have much sympathy for white girls. And I'm remembering what my mama told me, and I'm remembering the picture of that boy they pulled out of the Tallahatchie, sweet smiling boy like I was then, fourteen years old and a white girl's picture in his wallet, so he don't think nothing of being friendly with a white woman in a store. Then the other picture—skull crushed, eye gouged out, only the ring on his finger to tell his mama who he was, everything else that was his boy's life gone: cocky grin, sleepy eyes, felt hat, his skinny-hipped way of walking, all that gone, dragged to the bottom of the river by a cotton-gin fan tied to his neck with barbed wire. Mama said she wasn't trying to turn me mean but she wanted me to see—for my own good—because she loved me, which is why she did everything—because she'd die if anything happened to me—and I thought, even then, something was bound to happen, sooner or later, the fact of living in my black skin a crime I couldn't possibly escape. I only had to look once for one second to carry him around with me the rest of my life, like a photograph in my back pocket that didn't crack or fade, that just got sharper instead, clear as glass and just as dangerous till I pulled it out one day and realized I'd been staring at myself all those years.

I thought about that boy when I met Rita. He breathed on my neck and I laughed to make him stop. I didn't go after her. It was nothing like that. It was just something that happened—like the white girl pounding at my door—I was watching it, then I was in it.

We were at Wally's, me and Leo Stokes, listening to the music, jazz—we liked the music. Mostly I'm listening to the drummer thinking he don't got it right. He thinks he's too important. He don't know the drums are supposed to be the sound underneath the sound. That's why I'm good—that's why I want to play—I got a gift. I hear a sound below horn and piano, the one they need, like I did back in Virginia living in one room—Mama and Daddy, Bernice and Leroy and me, and there were lots of sounds all the time, but I'm always listening for the one sound—like at night when Mama and Daddy are fighting and her voice keeps climbing higher and higher like it's gonna break, and his is low and hard and slow, and then they're tangled together and the words don't make sense, but I'm not scared—no matter how bad it gets—because I'm listening. I hear a whippoorwill or grasshoppers, the wings of cicadas in July, a frenzy of wings rubbing, trying to wear themselves down, and I know what they want—I know what we all want—and it's like that sound is holding everything else together, so even if Mama starts crying, and even if Daddy leaves and don't come back till afternoon the next day, and even if they stop arguing and the other sounds start, even if Daddy has to put his hand over Mama's mouth and say, *Hush now, the children,* even if they get so quiet I can't hear their breathing, I know everything's okay and I'm safe, because the cicadas are out there, and they've been there all along, even when I didn't know I was hearing them, that one sound's been steady, that one sound's been holding everything tight. So I'm listening to the music, thinking, This drummer don't know his place. He thinks he's got to get on top of things. And I hear Leo say, *Luck or trouble, little brother, heading this way,* and then she's there, standing too close, standing above me. She's saying, *Spare a cigarette?* She's whispering, *Got a light?* And then she's sitting down with us and she's got her hand on my hand while I light her cigarette and I'm thinking she's pretty—in a way, in this light—and she's older, so I think she knows things—and I ask myself what's the harm of letting her sit here, and that's when I laugh to make the boy's breath and my mama's voice go away.

Then later that night I'm looking at my own dark hand on her thin white neck and it scares me, the difference, the color of me, the size, and she says, *What color is the inside of your mouth, the inside of your chest?* She says, *Open me—do I bleed, do my bones break?* She says, *Kiss me, we're the same.* And I do. And we are. When we're alone, we are.

She came to see me once. Cried, said she was sorry, and I sat there looking like I had stones in my stomach, ashes in my chest, like I didn't want to put my hands around her neck to touch that damp place under her hair. I told myself, She's not so pretty anymore. She looked old. The way white women do. Too skinny. Cigarettes and sun making her skin crack. Purple marks dark as bruises under her green eyes. I said, *Look, baby, I'm tired, you get on home.* I'm acting like I can't wait to get back to my cell, like I'm looking forward to the next three thousand nights smelling nothing but my own rotten self, like I've got some desire to spend nine years looking at the bodies of men, like I haven't already wondered how long it's gonna be before I want them. She says she didn't know, she didn't mean to make it worse for me, and I say, *Where you been living, girl? What country?* She's not crying then, she's pissed. She says, *You know what they did to me when I came in here? You know where they touched me?* And I say, *One day. One friggin' hour of your life. I live here, baby. They touch me all the time. Whenever they want. Wherever.*

I'm not saying she stuck the needle in my arm and turned me into a thief. I'm saying I wasn't alone. Plenty of things I did I shouldn't have. I paid for those. Three burglaries, nine years, you figure. So yeah, I paid for a dozen crimes they never slapped on me, a hundred petty thefts. But the man don't mind about your grandfather's gold pocket watch; he don't worry when the ten-dollar bill flies out of your mama's purse and floats into your hand. He don't bother you much if he sees you shoving weed on your own street. But that was different. Back when I was peddling for Leo I had a purpose, doing what I had to do to get what I needed. Then things turned upside down with Rita, and I was robbing my own mama, stealing to buy the dope instead of selling it, smack instead of grass. Rita said: *Just once—you won't get hooked, and it's fine, so fine, better than the music, because it's inside.* She was right—it was better than the music, and it was inside: it made me forget the sound and the need.

Now my mama is singing me to sleep, humming near my ear, *Bless the child,* and I'm waking as a man twenty-one years old, and I'm going to Walpole till I'm thirty. Sweet-faced Rita has scrubbed herself clean for the trial. She says it was all my idea and she was afraid, who wouldn't be? Seven men see their own wives, their own daughters, and pray no man like me ever touches their pretty white things. They think they can put me away. They think locked doors and steel bars keep them safe. Five women see their own good selves and swear they'd never do what Rita did if not by force.

I want to tell them how different she can be, how she looks when she's strung out, too jittery to talk, when her jaw goes so tight the tendons pop in her neck. I want to tell them how she begged me, *Please Jimmy please,* how she said it was so easy, her old neighborhood, her own people, habits she could predict, dogs she could calm. I want to ask them, *Do black men drive your streets alone?* I want to tell them, *I was in the back, on the floor, covered by a blanket. She drove. She waited in the car, watching you, while I broke windows, emptied jewelry boxes, hunted furs.*

Next thing I know I'm in prison and she's on probation and Mama's telling me, *You got to stay alive.* Ninety-two times she says it. Once a month for eight years, then one month she doesn't show, and the next week Bernice comes, says Mama's sick and aren't I ashamed. Then Mama comes again, three more times, but she's looking yellowish, not her high yellow but some new dirty yellow that even fills her eyes. She's not losing her weight but it's slipping down around her in strange ways, hanging heavy and low, so when she walks toward me, she looks like a woman dragging her own body. *My baby.* That's all she says. But I know the rest. Then Bernice is there again, shaking her head, telling me one more time how Mama gave up her life to give us a decent chance and she's got reason to be proud—little Leroy a schoolteacher, Bernice a nurse. I mean to remind her, *You feed mashed-up peas to old ladies with no teeth. You slip bedpans under wrinkled white asses. Wearing a uniform don't make you no nurse, Bernice.* But I just say, *Lucky for Mama the two of you turned out so fine.* I grin but Bernice isn't smiling; Bernice is crossing her big arms over her big chest. I see her fall to her knees as if her body is folding under her. I see her face crumple as if she's just been struck. And I'm not in prison. I'm free, but just barely, and I see my own dark hands in too-small white gloves, five other men like me, lifting the box and Mama in it, the light through stained glass breaking above us and that terrible wailing, the women crying but not Mama, the women singing as if they still believe in their all merciful God, as if they've forgotten their sons: sacrificed, dead, in solitary, on the street, rotting in a jungle, needles in their arms, fans tied around their necks, as if they don't look up at Jesus and say, *What a waste.*

I remembered my own small hands in the other white gloves; I thought my skin would stain them. The bull was dead. I would never be washed clean. But I was, baptized and redeemed. The white robes swirled, dragged me down, blinded me, and I thought, I can't swim, I'm going to die, and this is why my father wouldn't come to church today—the preacher in black is letting me die, is holding my head under—he wants me to die, it's necessary—I remember the stories my mother and I read, forbidden stories, our secret: cities crumbling, land scorched, plagues of frogs and gnats, plagues of boils and hail, seas and rivers turned to blood, and then, suddenly, I am rising and I am alive, spared by grace. The whole church trembles around me, women singing, telling Moses to let their people go, sweet low voices urging the children to wade in the water, but I know it's too deep, too dark, and I wasn't wading, I was drowning, but the voices are triumphant, the walls are tumbling down. Easter morning light blazes through colored glass; John baptizes Jesus above the water where we are baptized. I am shivering, cold, crying. Mama is sobbing, too; I hear her voice above the others, but I know she's happy. I know that Jesus is alive again just as I am alive, and I have never been this clean, and I am going to be good forever, and I am going to love Jesus who has saved me through his suffering, and I am going to forgive my father who has forsaken me. I am high and righteous and without doubt. I am ten years old.

These same women are still singing about that same damn river, like this time they're really going to cross it, when everybody knows they're stuck here just like me and not one of us can swim; the only river we see is thick as oil and just as black, so what's the point of even trying when you'd be frozen stiff in two minutes and sinking like the bag of sticks and bones you are, and still they won't stop swaying, as if they have no bones, as if the air is water and they are under it, and they are swimming, and they cannot be drowned, as if women have a way of breathing that men don't. I'm choking. I look at Leroy to see if he's drowning, too, to see if he's gasping, remembering Mama, our love for her, our guilt, but he's not guilty, he's a good clean boy, a teacher, clever little Leroy making numbers split in pieces, making them all come together right again. *Nothing can be lost,* he says, and he believes it. I say, *Didn't you ever want anything?* And he looks at me like I'm talking shit, which I suppose I am, but I still wonder, *Why didn't you feel it, that buzz in your veins, the music playing; why didn't you ever close your eyes and forget who it was Mama told you not to touch? Didn't we have the same blind father? Didn't you ever wonder where Mama got her gold eyes? Didn't the rabbit-man ever fly through your open window?*

Twenty years now and I still want to ask my brother the same questions. Twenty years and I still want to tell our mama I'm sorry—but I know there are times *sorry* don't mean a thing. I want to ask her, *Do you blame me?* And I want to ask her, *Should I go out in the snow?* I almost hear her answer, but I don't go.

Digging graves, hauling garbage, snaking sewers—I've done every filthy job, and now, two years, something halfway decent, graveyard shift but no graves. It's good work, steady, because there are always broken windows, busted doors. Fires burst glass; cars jump curbs; bullets tear through locks; police crack wood—always—so I don't have to worry, and Mama would be proud.

I'm alone with it, boards and nails, the hammer pounding. I strike straight, hold the place in my mind, like Daddy said. It's winter. My bare hands split at the knuckles, my bare hands bleed in the cold. Wind burns my ears but I don't mind. I don't want anything—not money, not music, not a woman. I know how desires come, one hooked to the other, and I'm glad my heart is a fist, shattered on a prison wall, so I don't have to think I might still play—because I can't, and it's not just the bones broken. But sometimes I hear the sound underneath the sound: it's summer, it's hot, the radios are blasting—brothers rapping, Spanish boys pleading, bad girls bitching—nobody knows a love song—then the gun goes off, far away, and I hear that, too, and later, sirens wailing. There's an argument downstairs, the Puerto Rican girl and her Anglo boyfriend, cursing in different languages. All those sounds are the song, pieces of it, but I'm listening for the one sound below it all, the one that pulls us down, the one that keeps us safe. Then I catch it: it's the rain that's stopped—it's the cars passing on the wet street—it's the soft hiss of tires through water, and it almost breaks me.

If I could find Rita now I'd tell her she was right: junk is better than jazz. It's fast and it doesn't hurt you the way the music does. It's easy. It takes you and you don't have to do anything. It holds you tighter than you've ever been held. You think it loves you. It knows where to lick and when to stop. When it hums in your veins, it says, *Don't worry, I'm with you now.*

I'd tell her, The blues scare everybody. They make you remember things that didn't happen to you, make you feel your bones aren't yours only—they've been splintered a thousand times; the blood has poured out of you your whole life; the rabbitman's skin is your skin and the body you share is on fire. Or it's simpler than that, and you're just your own daddy, or your own mama sitting beside him. Then you wish you didn't have to feel what they feel, and you get your wish, and you're nobody but your own self, watching.

Every beat I played was a step closer to my uncle's house where I listened to my cousins breathe in the bed above me, where I slept on the floor because Daddy was blind in our house, Daddy's legs were swollen twice their size and stinking, Daddy was cut loose on his own poison and Mama was there, alone, with him—giving him whiskey, washing him, no matter what he said, no matter who he cursed.

My cousins take me to the woods, Lucy and Louise, one older, one younger; they say, *Touch me here, and here.* They dare me, they giggle. They touch *me* and make me forget what's happening across the field, in my house; then they run away and I hear the grasshoppers chirping all around me, buzzing—frantic, invisible—and then, I remember.

But smack, it makes you forget, it makes you not care, just like Rita said. It promises: *There's nothing more you need to know.* So I didn't have to see my father's never-clean clothes snapping on the line. I didn't have to remember Mama bent over the washtub in the yard, flesh of her arm quivering like she wanted to wash out evil as well as filth. I didn't have to go in the truck with Daddy that morning when he said it was time I saw my future. I didn't have to swing the sledgehammer with my boy's arms or see the bull's eyes, mad with disbelief.

But now I remember everything, how I struck the head but too close to the nose, so there was the crack, and blood spouting from the mouth but no crumpling, and Daddy said: *Hold the place in your mind.* I swung a second time, grazed the face, and the bull swelled with his own breath, filling the stall. Three strikes in all before my father grabbed the hammer: one blow, and the animal folded, knees bending, neck sagging, the whole huge beast collapsing on itself.

Then the others came, sawed off head and legs, slit skin from flesh, peeled the animal—*strange fruit*—and there was blood, a river of it, hot, and there was blood, swirling at my feet. The body opened and there was blood weeping from the walls and the rabbitman ran so fast he ran out of his own skin and the bowels spilled, an endless rope, thick and heavy, full, and the smell, but the men work in the heat of the animal: kidneys, bladder, balls— saved, and the blood spatters them: faces, hands, thighs—they are soaked with it, I am soaked; I will never be clean, and even the ceiling is dripping until at last the carcass is hung on a hook in the cold room full of bodies without legs or heads or hearts.

But I am washed clean and I do forgive my father and my father dies and my grandparents forgive my mother for her bad marriage. I am fifteen. It's November, still warm in Virginia but not in Boston, which is where we're going, on the train, with my grandfather, who is kind enough but doesn't know us, who won't come inside our house, who's brought a suitcase full of clothes we have to wear and shoes that hurt our feet. He and Granny Booker mean to save us, mean to *compensate.* They say we can be anything. But all I want to be is the music, all I want to hear is the sound. Doctor Booker means I can be like him, and I think about that, the sharp razor's edge of his scalpel, all his delicate knives. I feel his clamps. I touch speculum and forceps, imagining how precisely he opens the body, what he finds there when he does. I see the familiar brown spatters on shirt cuffs and pant legs, his never-clean clothes, and I think, For all your pride, you're no better than my father, no different, and the distance from his house to yours is only the space it takes a man to turn around.

I remember my father crying. It frightened me more than anything, more than the bull, more than the water where I thought I'd drown. And this is all it was: scarecrow on a fence. He must have been going blind even then. He thought it was another one, body tangled in barbed wire. But it was only clothes stuffed with rags, pillowcase head tied off at the neck, straw hat and empty sleeves blowing in hot wind.

In prison I learned that my body itself is the enemy, my skin so black it reflects you. You want to take it from me. I terrify. Even when I am one and you are twenty. Even when I am cuffed and you have clubs. Even when I show you my empty hands and you show me your guns. I alarm you. I do what any animal will do: no matter how many times you strike, I try to stand. I mean to stay alive.

Which is why the girl in the street scared me. I thought, Maybe she's not a crackhead. Maybe she's just a woman from the other side, lost in another country, running deeper into it because once you're here you can't see your way out. Cross a road; walk under a bridge; that's how far. No signs, no stone wall, but the line is tight as a border crossing. If you close your eyes it glitters like broken glass, pale and blue, a thousand shattered windshields. Here, every gesture is a code. Boys patrol their turf, four square blocks, pretend they own something. They travel in packs and arm themselves because they're more afraid than any of us, because every time they look up the sky is falling, so they're rapping about the cops they're gonna dust, the cities they're gonna torch. The little brothers are spinning on their heads, like this is some dance, some game—their bodies twist in ways they were never meant to bend, and then everybody in the street just falls down dead.

And the old men like me sit in the bars, drinking whiskey, going numb, talking about snatch and getting even all in the same breath, and we sound just like our own pitiful mamas, saying: *Judgment Day gonna come, righteous gonna be raised up, and the wicked gonna suffer, rich or poor, don't make no difference.* Except the men, the justice they're talking don't have nothing to do with God. They're full of the old words, saying, *We can't come in the house we're gonna knock it down;* then they sound just like the boys in the street, only tired and slurred, and the boys out there, they're quick, they got matches and gasoline, they talk fast as spit and don't ever need to sleep. But the flames burst at their backs, and they're the ones on fire.

We know the rules. Mess with white folks, you pay. Kill a white man, you hang. Kill a black man? That's just one more nigger off the street. So when I think about that girl, when I think, If she's still out there, she's in trouble, when I think even my mama would tell me I should go, I remind myself: I already done enough time for a white girl. I know how they are, how she'd be scared of me even if I said, *I just want to help you.* And I know how it would look in the alley—big black man's got his hands on a skinny white girl. Just my luck the boyfriend would come looking, shoot me dead. Nobody'd ask him why.

I think, Maybe she's already dead and I'll find her, touch her once and leave the perfect print of my hand burned on her thigh. I don't have a phone and anyway, too late to call. They'd wanna know, *Why'd you wait so long,* and I'd be gone.

Last time they found a white woman dead on this hill police turned into a lynch mob, got the whole city screaming behind them. Roadblocks and strip searches. Stopped every dark-skinned man for miles if he was tall enough and not too old. Busted down doors, emptied closets, shredded mattresses, and never did find the gun that was already in the river. But they found the man they wanted: tall, raspy voice, like me. He's got a record, long, shot a police officer once. He's perfect. He can be sacrificed. No education, string of thefts. Even his own people are glad to turn him over, like there's some evil here and all we got to do is cut it out. I'm thinking, Nobody kills the woman and leaves the man alive. Even an ignorant nigger. But the police, they don't think that way. They need somebody. Turns out the husband did it. Shot his wife. Pregnant, too. Months later, white man jumps, bridge to river, January, he's dead, then everybody knows. But that black guy, he's still in jail. Violating parole. Some shit like that. Who knows? They got him, they're gonna keep him.

I hear two voices, and they both sound like my mama. One tells me, *She's human, go.* And one whispers, *You got to keep yourself alive.* One's my real mama and one a devil with my mama's voice.

Something howled. I thought it was the wind. I wanted to lean into it, wrap my arms around it. I wanted it to have a mouth, to swallow me. Or I wanted to swallow it, to cry as it cried, loud and blameless.

It was nearly dawn and I was ashamed, knowing now which voice belonged to my mama. I held the girl in my mind. She was light as a moth, bright as a flame. I knew she was dead. It was as if she'd called my name, my real one, the one I didn't know until she spoke it. I felt her lungs filling under my hand. She said: *There's one warm place at the center of my body where I wait for you.*

Stray finds her. Mangy wolf of a dog. Smells her. Even in this cold, he knows. And it's like he loves her, the way he calls, just whining at first, these short yelps, high and sad, and when nobody comes he starts howling, loud enough to wake the dead, I think, but not her. And it's day, the first one.

We're out there in the cold, nine of us in the alley, hunched, hands in pockets, no hats, shivering, shaking our heads, and one guy is saying, Shit, *shit,* because he remembers, we all remember, the last time.

I see her, close, thirty-five at least but small, so I thought she was a girl, and I think of her that way now. I kneel beside her. Her eyes are open, irises shattered like blue glass. Wind ruffles her nightgown, exposes her. Snow blows through her hair, across bare legs, between blue lips. I see bruises on her thighs, cuts on her hands, a face misaligned, and I think, I have bones like these, broken, healed, never the same. My hand aches in the cold.

I know now what happened, why she's here. I see her keeper. She smokes his cigarettes, he whacks her. She drinks his beer, he drags her to the toilet, holds her head in the bowl. He's sorry. I've heard the stories. I've seen the women. And I've been slammed against a cement wall for looking the man in the eye. I've been kicked awake at three a.m. because some motherfucker I offended told the guards I had a knife. The keepers make the rules, but they're always shifting: we can't be good enough.

Police stay quiet. Don't want to look like fools again. And nobody's asking for this girl. Stray, like the dog. They got time.

I know now what her body tells them: stomach empty, liver enlarged, three ribs broken, lacerations on both hands—superficial wounds, old bruises blooming like yellow flowers on her back and thighs. Death by exposure. No crime committed here. And they don't care who cut her, and they don't care who broke her ribs, because all her people are dead or don't give a shit, and she was the one, after all, who ran out in the snow, so who's to say she didn't want to die.

I drink port because it's sweet, gin because it's bitter, back to back, one kills the taste of the other. I can't get drunk. Three days now since we found her and I see her whole life, like she's my sister and I grew up with her. She's a child with a stick drawing pictures in the dirt. She's drawn a face and I think it must be her own face but I say, *What are you drawing;* and she says, *Someone to love me.* I say, *What are you trying to do, break my heart?* And she says, *If you have a heart, I'll break it.* I say, *Where's your mama?* And she says, *She's that pretty lady with red lips and high heels—you've probably seen her—but sometimes her lipstick's smeared all down her chin and her stockings are ripped and she's got one shoe in her hand and the spike is flying toward me—that's my mother.* I say, *Where's your daddy?* And she says, *He's a flannel shirt torn at the shoulder hanging in the closet ever since I've been alive and my mother says, That's the reason why.*

Then I see she's not a child; she's a full-grown woman, and her hands are cut, her hands are bleeding, and I say, *Who did this to you?* She won't answer, but I know, I see him, he's her lover, he's metal flashing, he's a silver blade in the dark, and she tries to grab him but he's too sharp. Then she's running, she's crying, and I see her in the street, and I think she's just some crazy white girl too high to feel the cold, and I don't go.

Now she's talking to me always. She's the sound underneath all other sounds. She won't go away. She says, *I used to make angels in the snow, like this; I used to lie down, move my arms and legs, like this, wings and skirt, but that night I was too cold, so I just lay down, curled into myself, see, here, and I saw you at your window, and I knew you were afraid, and I wanted to tell you, I'm always afraid, but after I lay down I wasn't so cold, and I was almost happy, and I was almost asleep, but I wanted to tell you, I'm your little white sister—I know you—we're alone.*

Cows

for Dermot Seymour

Even as we speak, there's a smoker's cough
from behind the whitethorn hedge: we stop dead in our tracks;
a distant tingle of water into a trough.

In the past half-hour—since a cattle truck
all but sent us shuffling off this mortal coil—
we've consoled ourselves with the dregs

of a bottle of Redbreast. Had Hawthorne been a Gael,
I insist, the scarlet *A* on Hester Prynne
would have stood for "Alcohol."

This must be the same truck whose taillights burn
so dimly, as if caked with dirt,
three or four hundred yards along the boreen

(a diminutive form of the Gaelic *bóthar,* "a road,"
from *bó,* "a cow," and *thar*
meaning, in this case, something like "athwart,"

"boreen" has entered English "through the air"
despite the protestations of the *O.E.D.*):
why, though, should one taillight flash and flare

then flicker-fade
to an afterimage of tourmaline
set in a dark part-jet, part-jasper or -jade?

That smoker's cough again: it triggers off from drumlin
to drumlin an emphysemantiphon
of cows. They hoist themselves onto their trampoline

and steady themselves and straight away divine
water in some far-flung spot
to which they then gravely incline. This is no Devon

cow-coterie, by the way, whey-faced, with Spode
hooves and horns: nor are they the metaphysicattle of Japan
that have merely to anticipate

scoring a bull's-eye and, lo, it happens;
these are earth-flesh, earth-blood, salt of the earth,
whose talismans are their own jawbones

buried under threshold and hearth.
For though they trace themselves to the kith and kine
that presided over the birth

of Christ (so carry their calves a full nine
months and boast liquorice
cachous on their tongues), they belong more to the line

that's tramped these cwms and corries
since Cuchulainn tramped Aoife.
Again the flash. Again the fade. However I might allegorize

some oscaraboscarabinary bevy
of cattle there's no getting round this cattle truck,
one light on the blink, laden with what? Microwaves? Hi-fis?

Oscaraboscarabinary: a twin, entwined, a tree, a Tuareg;
a double dung-beetle; a plain
and simple hi-firing party; an off-the-back-of-a-lorry drogue?

Enough of Colette and Céline, Céline and Paul Celan:
enough of whether Nabokov
taught at Wellesley or Wesleyan.

Now let us talk of slaughter and the slain,
the helicopter gunship, the mighty Kalashnikov:
let's rest for a while in a place where a cow has lain.

ROBERT CREELEY

Roman Sketchbook

As you come and go
from a place you sense
the way it might seem
to one truly there as
these clearly determined persons
move on the complex spaces

and hurry to their obvious
or so seeming to you
destinations. "Home," you think,
"is a place still there for all,"
yet now you cannot
simply think it was

or can be the same. It
starts with a small
dislocating ache, the foot
had not been that problem,
but you move nonetheless
and cannot remember the word

for foot, *fuss, pied*? some
thing, a childhood pleasure
she said she could put her
foot in her mouth but
that way is the past again,
someone's, the graying air

looks like evening here, the
traffic moves so densely,

you push close to the walls
of the buildings, the stinking
cars, bikes, people push by.
No fun in being one here,

you have to think. You must
have packed home in mind,
made it up, and yet all
people wait there, still patient
if distracted by what happens.
Out in the night the lights

go on, the shower has cleared the air.
You have a few steps more to the door.
You see it open as you come up, triggered
by its automatic mechanism, a greeting
of sorts, but no one would think of that.
You come in, you walk to the room.

IN THE CIRCLE

In the circle of an
increased limit all
abstracted felt event now

entered at increasing distance
ears hear faintly eye sees
the fading prospects and in-

telligence unable to get the
name back fails and posits
the blank. It largely moves

as a context, habit of being
here as *there* approaches, and
one pulls oneself in to prepare

for the anticipated slight shock—
boat bumping the dock, key
turning in lock, the ticking clock?

APOSTROPHE

Imaginal sharp distances we
push out from, confident
travelers, whose worlds are
specific to bodies— Realms of
patient existence carried without
thought come to unexpected end
here where nothing waits.

HERE

Back a street is the sunken
pit of the erstwhile market
first century where the feral

cats now wait for something
to fall in and along the
far side is the place where

you get the bus, a broad
street divided by two
areas for standing with a

covered provision, etc. *Antichi!*
Zukofsky'd say—all of it
humbling age, the pitted, pitiful

busts someone's sprayed with blue
paint, the small streets laboring
with compacted traffic, the generous

dank stink floods the evening air.
Where can we go we will not
return to? Each moment, somewhere.

READING / RUSSELL SAYS, "THERE IS
NO RHINOCEROUS IN THIS ROOM"

Wittgenstein's insistence to Russell's
equally asserted context of world as
experienced *things* was it's *propositions*
we live in and no "rhinoceros" can
proceed other than fact of what so states
it despite you look under tables or chairs
and open all thinking to prove there's
no rhinoceros here when you've
just brought it in on a plate
of proposed habituated *meaning*
by opening your mouth and out it pops.

ELEVEN A.M.

Passionate increase of particulars
failing passage to outside formulae
of permitted significance who cry
with foreign eyes out there the
world of all others sky and sun
sudden rain washes the window
air fresh breeze lifts the heavy
curtain to let the room out into
place the street again and people.

IN THE ROOMS

In the rooms of building James
had used in *Portrait*
of a Lady looking up to
see the frescoes and edging

of baroque seeming ornament
as down on the floor we are

still thinking amid the stacks
of old books and papers, racks,
piles, aisles of patient quiet
again in long, narrow,
pewlike seated halls for
talking sit and think of it.

HOW LONG

How long
to be here
wherever
it is—

I THINK

I think
the steps up
to the flat
parklike top

of the hill by the Quirinale look
like where I'd walked when
last here had stopped
before I'd gone in

down to the Coliseum's
huge bulk
the massed rock
and the grassed plot

where the Christians fought
and the traffic roars round
as if time
only were mind

or all this
was reminiscence
and what's real
is not.

ROOM

World's become shrunk to
square space high ceiling
box with washed green
sides and mirror the eye
faces to looks to see the
brown haired bent head
red shirt and moving pen
top has place still apparent
whatever else is or was.

OUTSIDE

That curious arrowed sound up
from plazalike street's below
window sun comes in through
small space in vast green drapes
opened for the air and sounds
as one small person's piercing cry.

WALK

Walk out now as if
to the commandment
go forth or is it
come forth "Come out
with your hands up..."
acquiescent to each step.

WATCHING

Why didn't I call to the
two tense people passing us
sitting at the edge of the plaza
whom I knew and had reason
to greet but sat watching them
go by with intent nervous faces the
rain just starting as they
went on while I sat with another
friend under large provided umbrella
finishing dregs of the coffee, watching?

VILLA CELIMONTANA

As we walk past crumbling
walls friend's recalling his
first love an American
girl on tour who then
stays for three months in
Rome with him then off
for home and when he
finally gets himself to
New York two years or more
later they go out in
company with her friend
to some place on Broadway
where McCoy Tyner's playing
and now half-loaded comfortable
the friend asks, "What part of
yourself do you express
when you speak English?"
Still thinking of it and me now
as well with *lire* circling my head.

THE STREET

All the various
members of the Italian
Parliament walking
past my lunch!

AS WITH

As with all such
the prospect of ending
gathers now friends take
leave and the afternoon
moves towards the end
of the day. So too mind
moves forward to its place
in time and *now,* one
says, *and now—*

OBJECT

The expandable enveloping flat flesh
he pulls in to center in hotel
room's safety like taking in
the wash which had flapped
all day in the wind. *In,* he
measures his stomach, *in* like
manner his mind, *in*side his
persistent discretion, way, *un-*
opened to anything by *im*pression . . .

. . . .

So often in such Romantic apprehension
he had wanted only to roam
but howsoever he weighed it or waited
whatsoever was "Rome" was home.

Angels and the Bars of Manhattan

for Bruce

What I miss most about the city are the angels
and the bars of Manhattan: faithful Cannon's and the Night Cafe;
the Corner Bistro and the infamous White Horse;
McKenna's maniacal hockey fans; the waitresses at Live Bait;
lounges and taverns, taps and pubs;
joints, dives, spots, clubs; all the Blarney
Stones and Roses full of Irish boozers eating brisket
stacked on kaiser rolls with frothing mugs of Ballantine.
How many nights we marked the stations of that cross,
axial or transverse, uptown or down to the East Village
where there's two in every block we'd stop to check,
hoisting McSorleys, shooting tequila and eight-ball
with hipsters and bikers and crazy Ukrainians,
all the black-clad chicks lined up like vodka bottles on Avenue B,
because we liked to drink and talk and argue,
and then at four or five when the whiskey soured
we'd walk the streets for breakfast at some diner,
Daisy's, the Olympia, *La Perla del Sur,*
deciphering the avenues' hazy lexicon over coffee and eggs,
snow beginning to fall, steam on the windows blurring the film
until the trussed-up sidewalk Christmas trees
resembled something out of Mandelstam,
Russian soldiers bundled in their greatcoats,
honor guard for the republic of salt. Those were the days
of revolutionary zeal. Haughty as dictators, we railed
against the formal elite, certain as Moses or Roger Williams
of our errand into the wilderness. Truly,
there was something almost noble
in the depth of our self-satisfaction, young poets in New York,
how cool. Possessors of absolute knowledge,
we willingly shared it in unmetered verse,
scavenging inspiration from Whitman and history and Husker Du,

from the very bums and benches of Broadway,
precisely the way that the homeless
who lived in the Parks Department garage at 79th Street
jacked in to the fixtures to run their appliances
off the city's live current. Volt pirates;
electrical vampires. But what I can't fully fathom
is the nature of the muse that drew us to begin with,
bound us over to those tenements of rage
as surely as the fractured words scrawled across the stoops
and shuttered windows. Whatever compelled us
to suspend the body of our dreams from poetry's slender reed
when any electric guitar would do? Who did we think was
    listening?
Who, as we cried out, as we shook, rattled, and rolled,
would ever hear us among the blue multitudes of Christmas
    lights
strung as celestial hierarchies from the ceiling? Who
among the analphabetical ranks and orders
of warped records and secondhand books on our shelves,
the quarterlies and *Silver Surfer* comics, velvet Elvises,
candles burned in homage to *Las Siete Potencias Africanas*
as we sat basking in the half-blue glimmer,
tossing the torn foam basketball nigh the invisible hoop,
listening in our pitiless way to two kinds of music,
loud and louder, anarchy and roar, rock and roll
buckling the fundament with pure, delirious noise.
It welled up in us, huge as snowflakes, as manifold,
the way ice devours the reservoir in Central Park.
Like angels or the Silver Surfer we thought we could
kick free of the stars to steer by dead reckoning.
But whose stars are they? And whose angels
if not Rilke's, or Milton's, even Abraham Lincoln's,
"the better angels of our nature" he hoped would emerge,
air-swimmers descending in apple-green light.
We worshipped the anonymous neon apostles of the city,
cuchifrito cherubs, polystyrene seraphim,
thrones and dominions of linoleum and asphalt:
abandoned barges on the Hudson mud flats;

Bowery jukes oozing sepia and plum-colored light;
headless dolls and eviscerated teddy bears
chained to the grills of a thousand garbage trucks; the elms
that bear the wailing skins of plastic bags in their arms all winter,
throttled and grotesque, so that we sometimes wondered
walking Riverside Drive in February or March
why not just put up cement trees with plastic leaves
and get it over with? There was no limit to our capacity for awe
at the city's miraculous icons and instances,
the frenzied cacophony, the democratic whirlwind.
Drunk on thunder, we believed in vision
and the convocation of heavenly presences summoned
to the chorus. Are they with us still? Are they
listening? Spirit of the tiny lights, ghost beneath the words,
numinous and blue, inhaler of bourbon fumes and errant shots,
are you there? I don't know. Somehow I doubt we'll ever know
which song was ours and which the siren
call of the city. More and more, it seems our errand
is to face the music, bring the noise, scour the rocks
to salvage grace notes and fragmented harmonies,
diving for pearls in the beautiful ruins,
walking all night through the pigeon-haunted streets
as fresh snow softly fills the imprint of our steps.
O.K., I'm repeating myself, forgive me, I'm sure brevity
is a virtue. It's just this melody keeps begging to be hummed:
McCarthy's, on 14th Street, where the regulars drink
beer on the rocks and the TV shows *Police Woman*
twenty-four hours a day; the quiet, almost tender way
they let the local derelicts in to sleep it off
in the back booths of the Blue & Gold after closing;
and that sign behind the bar at the Marlin, you know
the one, hand-lettered, scribbled with slogans of love and abuse,
shop-worn but still bearing its indomitable message
to the thirsty, smoke-fingered, mood-enhanced masses—
"Ice Cold Six Packs To Go." Now that's a poem.

JESSICA HAGEDORN

Black: Her Story

The Mexican Mother Meets the Oldest
Living Virgin of Manila

Queridisimo Doctorcito: Thank you for the foetus you sent me. The baby boy. Would you say I was a jazz poem, spit from the mouth of a saxophone? Or would you send me straight to hell? Pensamiento, pentimento, pimiento... Can you believe my mother is dead? And her twin sister? And my father, too? All within a matter of months, yet none of them liked each other. Here, then, my grocery list of fickle desires. Once again, I am. Your monkey. Your Frida.

Reddish-purple: Aztec. Old blood of prickly pear. The most alive and oldest color.
Black: Nothing is black. Really, nothing.

His story. Her story. I lose patience with the obvious and clench my fists. Imagine. Lim Ah Hong. Big Wong. Manong. All wrong. What my Mexican mother said before she died: *The joke of a dream. The red vision. I cannot tolerate morphine.* Forty years later, my Chinese brother says to my brother: *Oh, you Filipinos. You love us, you hate us, you kidnap us. But you can't live without us.*

Here's another version: "Oh, you Filipinos. Can't stop dreaming about us. Blame us, love us, hate us, kidnap our children, and kill us. Burn our houses down.... But you can't live without us."

Here's my version: "Oh, you Filipinos. You so fucked up."

What to do when the English no longer makes sense? *Ay, puta. Ay naku. Buwisit. Putang ina mo. Que asco. Que barbaridad. Que horror.*

Imagine. It is 1963 and I have just arrived here. You are still sitting on a mound of dirt over there, watched over by Jesuits. We curse in Tagalog, Spanish, English, Fukkienese, Mandarin. You study the faces of old immigrant men and women, terrified. You are not born yet. It is 1963. Soon, Kennedy and then Malcolm X will be assassinated. Does America live up or down to my expectations? Is it the Hollywood of our colonized imaginations? You are born. The Vietnam War is finally over. I am mistaken for a *pachuca* in high school. *You pachuco pachuca chicana greaser girl? Yeah, I say. Sure.*

What is a Filipino? Kinda like a Mexican, I say. But not really. How about this image: we're small-time gangsters who can dance. Yo-yo champions of the world. Isn't that an easy one for you to access? Oh, they say, disappointed. But. You speak English so well. How did you learn so much, swimming from island to island?

It is 1984 and you've just arrived. I don't know you yet, but we've met somewhere before—over there, I'm sure. I already know what you're going to say as the movie projector switches on in my head. Images that recur burn up the screen. *Let us begin.*

A woman nailed to a cross. Contrary to popular opinion, she is not bleeding.

A woman suspended in a red void. Her daughters float in the sky above her. She reaches out, her legs spread, the palms of her hands up in a gesture of...supplication? beseeching? blessing? Is she screaming or laughing? She is childless but imagines her children into existence. A profane, immaculate conception.

One daughter wears a red dress, as red as the red void in which her mother is suspended. The other daughter is a baby, a naked peach, a fierce olmec cherub. Like her sister in the scarlet dress, like her mother has taught her from the womb, the floating baby's eyes are shut in a constant dream. Her tiny, terrifying teeth are bared in a sly jaguar grin. She is beautiful. Her sister in the bloody dress is beautiful. A poet materializes into the frame. She is the mother's twin, a woman from Alhambra shrouded in black velvet.

Her glass bangles make too much noise, and the baby almost wakes up. "Look what you've done," the twins accuse each other.

The mother's legs scissor the red horizon. Her back splits open, magnolia, plumeria, and calla lilies unfurl on her broken spine. Her flesh a map of scars. A map of the universe. Manong, manong. Walk the dog. Stand still. Big Wong. What went wrong?

Dear Doctorcito. Find a soft spot, what's left of my skin, and inject. There. There. She has learned that what is possible is often not visible. She's a monkey. She devours bananas, crackers, and cheese. She pours hot wax on her bald, bent head. She howls even when she sleeps. She's a scammer, a thief, the queen of self-pity, the Empress of Sorrow. She paints everything gold. The stove, the refrigerator, the radio, the telephone, the bed, the plates, the silver. *Midasina, Medea, Medusa.* Jump cut. The twin sister poet holds up a tube of red lipstick. The mother sister puckers her lips. *Find a soft spot. There. There.* Mother, sister, daughter, daughter, sister, sister, niece, aunt. Twin. There are too many women in this house. A cluster of spikes, not snakes. The woman nailed to a cross grows bored with the nails embedded in her palms, embedded in her beautifully manicured feet. There is no blood. The nails are brand-new, rustproof. Dipped in hydrogen peroxide before being hammered in. She grows bored with her anguish, screeches with rage and writhes for her salvation. Her children howl along with her, a chorus of thorns

"Somebody yank this shit out."

There is too much light in the room. The movie abruptly ends.

Imagine. The Philippine landscape lit by a pale gold moon. You've been there. We were born in a cemetery, a tropical burial ground made unholy by Christian generals, immortal tyrants, and their lacquered wives. Your mother's ghost dances on a piano in a haunted house in Sarrat. Your father gasps for breath and jabs at the air with a knife. It is you he wants. Mine gasps for air and weeps like a child in that hospital in Makati. Like yours, he's been dying for years. Love him, hate him, burn his house down.

Your mother shrieks with joy: *So much gold it lights up the night!*
Our mothers... whose pleasures were Catholic, forbidden, and
therefore fleeting.

Knock knock. Who's there? Emy. Emy who? Emygrant. A diva I once
knew defined motherhood as "the ultimate censorship." On the
telephone, I can't tell her voice apart from her daughter's. It's the
main reason I don't call her anymore.

Imagine. Delicious obsessions. You flew here on an airplane. I
sailed on a ship. Magellan went looking for spices. All those mad
Europeans went looking for spices. Their lives lacked chili pepper
and heat, they longed for something they could not name, what
was possible was not visible, so in the name of God & the Fat Pale
Queen they went sailing in search of gold, pepper, saffron, cinnamon, and souls. And here we are, the bastards of Discovery, quin-
centennial years later! You flew here on an airplane. You flew here
in a rage. I sailed on a ship for an eternity of seventeen days to
California, and shut my eyes to save myself and dream. *Little
Richard, Chuck Berry, Fats Domino...*

Bad vibes back home. In my dream, the natives throw a fiesta but
they smell something fishy. For once, they aren't buying into it—
not the blue-eyed priest, not the startling skin, not the gold of the
conquistador's hair or the gold of his cross, not the smell or shape
or shine of any of it. It is 1521 on the island of Mactan. The air
stinks of paranoia, Spanish sweat, and death. No one's feeling
hospitable. Unlike Columbus, Magellan gets dissed, ambushed,
and decapitated. WHACKED off by the tribal chief Lapu Lapu,
Magellan's head rolls on and on and on across the bloody sand of
the beach and disappears into the salty Pacific ocean.

In the official version, the armor-suited Magellan is felled by
arrows and left to die on the beach. But I like mine better.

*How we remember. What we remember. Why? Who? What? Where?
When? Who? Who else? Who with? Who said? How? How much?
With what? With whom? Where else? Why? Why? Why? Why is the*

cross of Magellan a tourist attraction in the Philippines? Why is a scavenger fish named after Lapu Lapu in the Philippines?

O Ferdinand, O Isabella, O Cristofer, O Cortez, O Lopez de Legaspi, O Ponce, O Balboa, O Vasco de Gama, O Popes of manifest destiny. There was never enough gold to mine. This was never Peru, and all you found was cinnamon.

Wrong again. It is 1941 and I'm in my casita azul. I'm wearing your pants and smoking a cigarette. It's one I rolled myself, I'm terrible at rolling anything—the tobacco keeps falling out, the paper is soaked with saliva, and I keep having to relight the cigarette. But I look good, don't I? A pensive pose—*kalachuchi* flower stuck in my thick black hair... dead center, so you can't miss it in the photograph. The one where I stand next to Trotsky. Somber yet stunning. *Just so,* how I lean against the wall of my little blue house of skulls.

Did you decide early on if you were ugly or pretty? Were you considered a barrio beauty? You have to choose—it helps you endure. Filipinos know how to endure, don't they? *Magtiis ka lang,* we say. I decided early on that I was magnificent. I smoked my cigars, I wore my rustling skirts with their layers of ostentatious ruffles and itchy lace, I was Diego's sequined monkey bride with my sunflower headdress instead of a veil. The starched rays of my Tehuantepac crown jutting out from the sides of my head. I was your mother, goddammit, the leopard queen bitch of kitsch. I nag you from my grave, in my eternal agony glorious still.

And where are Dolores, Bessie, and Perlita? La Chinita Anna May? El maldito Nelson Rockefeller? And that fucking Maria Felix... how dare she outlive me!

Dear Doctorcito: I'm wearing my motorcycle jacket. The one that's black and smells of skin. Caimito de Guayabal is perched on my shoulder. Sweet monkey. I ape the ape Caimito, I'm your monkey perched on a pew. My moustache is waxed, my silver fur brushed and gleaming with Tres Flores pomade. The airless chapel is fra-

grant with my fecal perfume. My dainty black old lady hands are
clasped in prayer. Father. Hear my confession. Mother. Bless your
little monkey for I have sinned. Sin verguenza, your Jessica.

Dear Doctorcito. I want a shave, please. Give me a close shave. Don't
shave me too close. I am very thin-skinned.

Everything you made up is true. My brother exists. He's a twenti-
eth-century zealot on lithium, ranting the scriptures in Tagalog
and English to anyone who listens. No one does. *Cobalt blue: elec-*
tricity, pure love.

I'm a nun on fire, I wear your baggy pants, I'm Diego in love. Rub
my rotunda of a belly 3x for good luck. On your knees, you hob-
ble like a cripple from one station of the cross to the other. There
are exactly fourteen. Take your time. Don't ask too many questions. Keep the faith. The church is our motherfucker, this
abstract *ménage à trois* a sacred passion.

Where do we live now? Here or there? Are you disappointed?
Have your dreams and ways of speaking become too precise and
American?

Dear Doctorcito: Some say the yo-yo was invented by a Filipino.
Some say the Chinese. Why do they always say the Chinese? Some
say it once was a jungle weapon. Even the French have tried claim-
ing it as theirs. In English, yo-yo connotes flakiness. The back and
forth motion of indecision. A toy. In Spanish, yo-yo means "I, I."
I read somewhere that in Tagalog, yo-yo means "to return."

Beware of yellow. Frida defined it as the color of madness, sickness, fear. But also as the color of the sun, and joy. *Maginghat ka,*
ha. Maraming mga hayop duun...at dito rin, sa gabi...in the
night. While my daughters sleep, we'll laugh and steal each other's
words. Reinvent geography. Recall our flight from one shifting
continent to the next. Wallow in the mud of mistaken identities.
Cross-dress to Calvary.

Landscape with Coyote and Special Effects

At peace with all creatures not me
I incite a fireship to torch the horizon
with flamboyance pouring over blue snow
toward the mesa I stand on—out of a quirk

little nobler than phototropism,
and loving to see our morning world happen
and the centuries turn in my absence.
Among powdery drifts a distant coyote

snuffles, questing for field mice. Picks up
my slight motion. Pauses. Stock still. Gives me
that look they have: long, steady, practical.
Then curls away behind dusky junipers

as if well-advised. But who can feel shunned
by wind, wind lending brush and dumb boulders
a say in the matter? "Take it from us,"
they admonish. "Rest content in the heart's

great adventure of every time, and the wondrous
nothings it beats for." Cold air over red stone?
Surely that is the voice of experience
naming the warmest way we can be—if not how.

But I listen. Whereupon my sidereal
past gets into the act as an extravagant star
bedazzling the lashes. Its prodigal holocaust
ascends beyond knowing or ever caring to know,

"What have you done with your chances
and all that I lent you?" What indeed

if not years, orbiting the mystery
of my own existence, or anyone's; yet dawn

is near as I've come. When its reapparition
colors breath of the flying rock I was born on
my eyes often admit the full story: "Not enough.
Wrong things. And this."

Astrophysics

"Can't go on," sighed the heart taking leave
of its mind and throwing itself at the sun.

Ninety-three million miles in no time.

Past the mad gas of the solar corona
shot that hunk of red meat
meteoric—straight through the sun's bubble
to the wild interior, the fusion place.

Its molecules spat up their ghosts.
Its sad atoms sizzled apart
like blue bees, at last incandescently happy
to whiz into and fuse with the fine-boned
nuclei of helium, the iron ones rugged as trucks,
the affluent beryllium, bedizened with neutrons.

What on earth had the heart ever wanted
beyond helping each day tell its story?

If only the brain hadn't wondered so often
why those days had ever begun. Now their protons
went freely along with all they smacked into.
Now there was nothing they couldn't become,
red giant, white dwarf, down to eventual
densities smug as self-love: one pure
carbon star, many a million more times
single-minded than diamond.

"On the other hand..." flared the heart's
sanguine chambers—then retrofired
earthward in photons casual as pollen
back to the chest they had fled from.

At that the brain puzzled. "Once gone
why return? Yet why go in the first place?"

"Grown glum from scrubbing your moods,
solar envy crept into me, because the sun
never glimpses even one shadow, but I saw
only how lost we terrestrials are,
lacking shadow to see by,
and how willing the sun was
that I should still be your heart."

Looking at Kilauea

I've been looking at Kilauea
                    and its various eruptive features
for a few years now, and,
                    every time I do it,
I really never know what it is I'll be looking at,
looking for, remembering, or comparing it to.
It's kind of like daydreaming,
                    gazing at the birth-stem of all things.

    The looking follows the structure of a daydream,
                    finding its dips and turns,
its connections with the ten thousand things,
then dipping back again into a rapturous privacy
        and the specifics of the one that is before me—

a fissure line of rupture in the earth fuming with sulphurous air;
a glistening beach of newborn black sand;
a conical driblet spire crowning a fresh flow that,
                    out of its blowhole,
spouts an incandescent emission like red sperm over the new land;
solidified eddies of *paho'eho'e*
            swirled like fans of pandanus leaves
                    inundating Highway 130 near Kaimu;
or a frozen cascade of lava
            sluiced over a low, dun-colored bluff
that foregrounds a deep-focus panorama over the sublime,
        shades of gray and black plain of Ka'u Desert,
                    the mother's breast of my universe.

    When I first came here,
I was aware I was before a deep mystery
that shocked and yet seemed to work subtly too,
driving through the green thigh of imagination,

reminding me,
as my thoughts formed themselves
        into faintly tidal rhythms of realization and befuddlement,
of what was the quintessential mystery—
                        questions of poetry and creation.

My mind and soul seemed turning in a dance,
        squiring each other,
revolving like twin stars in a galaxy of lavas
    flowing in a slow, mortal spiral
up the bole of a frightened tree standing in its path,
        its crown a fan of gray coral,
                    creating a form out of fire and extinguishment,
a frothy, snakelike cone of astral matter,
blobs of yin and yang
                    in velocities of vortex and tango,
ascending up the blazing trunk of an *ohi'a* tree
                        burning to ash and char.

    I heard a song.
I had a little vision of schoolchildren crossing,
                        not a village green in London
or gamboling through some clichéd countryside
                    dotted with barns and farmponds,
but over a plain of smokes,
                    over a dire lake of black lavas
transformed into the congenial earth they could walk upon.

    There simply was everything to think about,
                    and my mind, in those moments,
seemed suddenly capable of thinking them all,
holding them in one breath's time,
the myriad of creation's entirety
caught in the spirit's dance of my apprehending.

An ocean of thoughts. A body made electric by them.

Death not ending, ever, but the absence of inspiration,
a falling from the bright light at the center of the earth.

Ralph Waldo Emerson wrote of this in his essay "Nature."
He spoke of crossing Concord Green at night
            with a feeling that removed him from himself,
taking in all of the universe
                        through the body of his soul,
which seemed to him like "a transparent eyeball."

His soul lifted.
All of learning, faith, and human effort
seemed subsumed in the momentary awareness.

What was Concord, Massachusetts, but a metaphor for human
      polity,
an earthly ambition, a city on a hill that looked upon heaven?

He resigned his ministry,
                  which had become, sadly,
            the fragmentation of his faith,
but his loyalty shifted
to the new mission of articulating his wonderfully homespun,
                        yet transcendental vision.

He wrote.
He became a poet,
            his testimonies given over to beauty.
            praising flowers,
                  a moment's thought,
the rhodora with eternity
            embowered deep in its blossoming pink cups.

   Living here,
            the looking gives details that, in the mind,
pile against each other like clouds against Mauna Loa,
subductions and effervescences shoring like seas against a
                              continent.
   Recollecting takes meditation,
                  another daydream, and then it comes:

   if I drove up from Wayne's house and through the park,

plunging past all the micro-climates of rain-beaded ginger lilies
and the scorched forest of *ohi'a* and staghorn ferns
dying in the suffocating sulfuric fogs of Steaming Bluffs,
crossing the little sink bowl of a tiny caldera matted with ferns
                                          and sedges,
I'd get to a mound of land near Uwekahuna
where I can look out over the inflatable summit dome of Kilauea
rising over a long slot of pulverized lavas, buff and brown in
                                          sunny weather.

If I stopped and pulled over,
if I walked out onto the little roll of the land
                    giving way to little faults and gullies,
                              an inner sea of unstable rock
                                    frequented with seismic swarms
                    and churning with a hundred rises
as if the gathering pods of khaki-backed, migrating whales
          were spuming their way from Kilauea Summit towards
                                          Mauna Loa,
I would see a long black groove
                    that would be Volcano Highway
twisting through the gully that is the seam of earthen creation
          where the land,
                              churning with perceptible movement,
becomes Mauna Loa,
                    an earthform "Concerto de Aranjuez"
building slowly through basaltic gradients of blue and gray
into the summit caldera obscured by clouds,
dwarfed by the inverted bowl of the afternoon sky's pale,
                                          porcelain blue.

I would lean against an onrush of wind
                    scudding over the plain of lavas,
sent by the flattening heel of a cloudbank,
                                          stratocumulus,
insubstantial wraith
          skydiving in the space between heaven and Kilauea,
between one volcano and another.

    If I reached beside me,
scrubby boughs of *ohelo* bushes would be cowlicking
like the thick fur between the shoulders of a wolf or a bear,
ruffled alert by wind or the scent of humans walking close-by.
Shining berries, some a deep red, others more pale,
                    some of them spotted with blemishes,
would bounce with a sugary weight against my hand
                          as I bent to pluck them.

The land and its atmosphere will have gathered themselves
into whatever act the clouds and myself might bring about:

                a tribute of afternoon rain,

garlands of purple trailing like a fringed skirt under the
                      moving clouds,
a handful of tiny fruit, unstrung,
           juicy pearls tossed from my hand
into the scuffed canyonlands of eroded lavas reaching out to me
                 from a sullen sleep,
the unimagined oblivion of dormancy, barren of praise.

I rouse this rock into the space of my own living.
It is music. It is the sweet scent of rain
        spouting in puffed quarternotes of dust on the land.

If I turned to leave.
        back toward my car parked by the side of the road,
I would be through with looking,
          my body shuffled against the wind
like a tree, red-brilliant,
        full of passionate blossoms too heavy for its boughs,
the long mountain at my back,
             pure upwelling of Kilauea in my soul,
the dancer and the dance,
        kin to earth again.

The Rights of Man

You could not call it an actual crucifixion, Doctor Hébert thought, because it was not actually a cross. Only a pole, or a log, rather, with the bark still on it and scars on the bark toward the top, from the chain that had dragged it to this place, undoubtedly. A foot or eighteen inches below the mark of the chain, the woman's hands had been affixed to the wood by means of a large square-cut nail. The left hand was nailed over the right, palms forward. There had been some bleeding from the punctures and the runnels of blood along her inner forearms had hardened and cracked in the dry heat, from which the doctor concluded that she must have been there for several hours at the least. Surprising, then, that she was still alive.

Alive and breathing in short sucking rasps, though her position would make it difficult to breathe. That would bring death, from suffocation, lungs crushed by the body's downward drag. Although her weight, depending from the vertex of the nail, must have pulled her diaphragm tight, the skin around her abdomen hung comparatively slack. At her pudenda appeared a membranous extrusion from which Doctor Hébert averted his eye. Her feet were transfixed one over the other by the same sort of homemade nail as held her hands.

Sitting on his horse, Doctor Hébert was at a level with her navel. He raised his head. Her skin was a deep, luminous black; he had become somewhat familiar with the shade since he had been in the country, but was not knowledgeable enough to place her origin from it. Her hair was cut close to the skull, which had the familiar angularity that the doctor, from the sculptural point of view, found rather beautiful. Her large lips were turned out and cracking in the heat, falling a little away from her teeth, and the look of them made the doctor's own considerable thirst seem temporarily irrelevant. When he had first ridden up, her eyes had shown only crescents of white, but now the lids pulled farther back and he knew that she was seeing him.

The elegantly contoured head hung over on her shoulder, twisting the cords of her neck up and out. He could see the big vein bumping slowly there. Her eyes moved, narrowing a little, at their sideways angle. She saw him, but was indifferent to what she saw. The doctor's tongue passed across his upper lip, once, twice, stiff as a file. He turned in the saddle and looked back into the long *allée* down which he had come. This avenue ran east to west for almost a mile, bordered by citrus trees whose branches had laced to the density of a thick hedge. From the far end of the *allée*, the pole had first appeared to him centered like the bead in a gunsight. Now the red round of the sun was dropping quickly into the notch where he had first entered, and the glare of it forced him to squint his eyes. He had gone astray some time that morning and had ridden through the afternoon over ill-made roads, if they were roads at all, without meeting anyone. When at last he came to the edge of the cane fields, he had called out to the cultivators there, but had not been able to understand what they said in reply.

Night came quickly in these parts. It might be dark before he could retrace his way to the other end of the *allée*. Doctor Hébert pressed a heel into his horse's flank and rode around the pole. The citrus trees, more sparsely set, fanned out around the edges of the compound as though they had meant to encircle it but failed. What vegetation there was looked completely untrained and much of the yard was full of dust. From one of the scattered outbuildings, a deep-voiced dog was barking. The doctor rode within a few yards of the long low building which was the *grand'case*, dismounted and walked the remaining distance to the pair of wooden steps to the gallery, where a white woman *en déshabillé* was sitting in a wooden chair with her head sunk down on her chest.

"Your pardon," Doctor Hébert said, mounting the first step.

The woman raised her head and rearranged her hands in her lap. In one hand she held a glass half full of a cool liquid with a greenish tint. "Oh," she said. "You have come."

The doctor stepped onto the planks of the gallery, removed his hat, and inclined his head. "I have a terrible thirst," he said. "I beg you."

"*Bien sûr,*" she said, and clapped her hands once sharply together. The doctor waited. His horse, waiting in the yard with the reins on its neck, lowered its head and snorted at the dust and raised it. There were steps from within and the doctor turned. A mulatto woman in a madras turban came scurrying out of the central door, carrying another glass, which she presented to the doctor with a sort of crouch. He took a long, rash gulp which made him gasp, and held the glass a little away from him to look at it. The concoction was raw cane rum with lime juice and a cloying amount of sugar. He finished the drink in several more cautious sips, while the white woman spoke to the mulattress in Creole.

"It is arranged," she finally said, turning back to the doctor, who now noticed that her eyes seemed a little bloodshot. "My husband..." Her head swung away as her voice trailed off. She looked out across the compound towards the pole.

"*Je vous remercie,*" Doctor Hébert said. There seemed no place to leave the glass; he stooped and set it on the floor. The horse shook its head as he approached. He took the reins and led it around the back of the *grand'case* and wandered among the outbuildings until he discovered the stable. At the rear of the roofed hall was a water trough made of an enormous dugout log. The horse drank and snuffled and blew onto the water and drank deeply again. The doctor watched its big throat working, then knelt and put two fingers into the trough. The water was cool and clear and he thought that it must often be replenished or changed. He cupped his hands and drank and ran his wet palms back over his hair. With a forefinger he detached a long, soggy splinter from the side of the trough and watched it drift loggily to the bottom.

A groom of some sort had appeared at his back but Doctor Hébert waved him away and led the horse to a stall himself, where he unsaddled it and gave it a bit of cane sugar from a cake he carried in the pocket of his duster. Slinging his saddlebags over his shoulder, he left the stable and walked back toward the *grand'case*.

The barking had taken up again and the doctor approached the shed it seemed to come from. When he put his eye to the crack in the door, a big brindled mastiff smashed against it, backed off, and lunged again, striking head-on into the wood with all its weight and force. The doctor withdrew abruptly and continued his path to the house.

A dark-haired man of middle height stood on the gallery. He wore a white shirt and breeches bloused into riding boots and he held a gold-pommeled cane in both hands across his thighs.

"*Bienvenu,*" he said, "to Habitation Arnaud. I myself am Michel Arnaud. You will dine here. You will pass the night."

"*Heureux,*" the doctor said, and bowed. "I am Antoine Hébert."

"Please to enter," Arnaud said, indicating the open doorframe with his cane. As the doctor passed through, another domestic relieved him of his saddlebags and carried them away through another doorway at the rear of the large central room. It was dim within, the oil paper over the windows admitting little of the fading light.

"In perhaps one hour we will go to table," Arnaud said. Standing at the outer doorway, he swatted his thigh with the cane. "You will wish to rest, perhaps."

"Yes," said Doctor Hébert. "Your people, they will feed my horse?"

"Immediately," Arnaud said, slapping himself once more with the cane as he turned farther out onto the gallery.

In the small room at the rear the slave had hung the doctor's saddlebags on a peg on the wall and stood waiting beside it, bobbing his head. He was barefoot and wore short pants and a loose shirt of the same coarse cloth and, incongruously, a black coat that looked as if it might have been cast off by the master.

"*De l'eau?*" Doctor Hébert said, without absolute expectation of being understood. The slave bowed out. Doctor Hébert hung his duster on the wall beside the saddlebags and sat down in a chair to remove his boots. His temples pounded when he straightened up; the rum undoubtedly contributing to this effect. In the room were one other wooden chair and a palliasse and one small oil-papered window. With a little clink, the slave set down a crockery pitcher and a cup on the floor, then backed out quietly, closing the door. Doctor Hébert poured a cup of water and drank it and lay down on his back. The papered window was no more than a pale patch dissolving slowly on the wall. After a time he became aware of the shifting of bare feet in the outer room. At the jingle of a little bell he got up and replaced his boots.

Four candles in heavy candlesticks were burning on the long table in the main room, and the table was laid with covers of silver and heavy imported *faïence*. Arnaud, standing at the head of the table, indicated to the doctor a place at his right. A slave drew back the chair and then adjusted it once the doctor had seated himself. The slave in the black coat, who seemed to fill some sort of butler's role, settled Arnaud in the same way, stepped back and waited. Above the table, a circular fan of boards began to move when a boy in a corner pulled a rope. At the end of the table opposite Arnaud, a fourth slave stood in attendance, although no place had been laid there.

"My wife is unable to join us at this moment," Arnaud said.

"She is unwell, perhaps," the doctor said, wondering if his glance had betrayed some false expectancy.

Arnaud stared at him. "*Pour un coup de tafia elle ferait n'importe quoi,*" he said. "*Alors, mangeons.*" At that, the slaves moved forward to lift the covers and present the several platters one by one. This burst of activity allowed the doctor to cover his moment of confusion. He had been on the point of offering his professional services, which evidently would not at all have done.

There was a highly seasoned platter of pork slices, a sort of ragout of sweet potatoes, nothing a-green. A bowl of pickle, one of jam, and a loaf of rather leaden bread. The wine was more than tolerable and Arnaud poured it liberally, or rather caused it to be poured, by making minute gestures with a finger. As always the doctor was slightly unnerved by the silent presence of the slave behind his chair; whenever he thought of reaching for anything on the table the slave would move to anticipate him.

Arnaud ate with dispatch, if not relish, and did not seem disposed to offer further conversation. In the candlelight his face had an olive tone. He had a weak chin, plump cheeks, and a small, plummy mouth like a woman's. In spite of the fan's agitation a sheen of sweat had appeared on his forehead. The doctor himself felt a little flushed, perhaps by the high seasoning of the food. He hoped most sincerely that he was not taking fever.

When the edge of his appetite was blunted he allowed his eyes to slide around the larger area of the room, though there was little for them to dwell on. Only the other doorways interrupted the walls; there were no pictures and no other ornament except for a large gilt-framed mirror. Toward the door to the gallery some more empty chairs were grouped around a low table made of local wood.

"We are very plain here," Arnaud said.

"Perhaps your stay is temporary," said Doctor Hébert. "You will make a great fortune and return to France."

"It seems unlikely that France will be any longer in existence when and if I ever amass a great fortune," Arnaud said. "News reaches us so slowly, it is more than possible that they have already burnt and murdered their way from one end of the country to the other at this moment, only we have yet to hear of it."

"I do not believe that matters are quite so desperate," the doctor said. "Although certainly it has been a very heady time."

"You may expect heads to be rolling down the public roads before this time is done," Arnaud said.

"Of course," the doctor said, "one hopes for a degree of moderation."

"I do not see that any middle course is viable," Arnaud said. "Not if the madmen in the National Assembly fall any further under the sway of Les Amis des Noirs. They understand nothing of the real conditions here. All this jabbering of liberty may be very well in France but among us it is nothing but incendiary. We will be brought to anarchy. Civil war. And worse." He snapped his fingers, and the three slaves moved to clear the table of the platters. When they had gone out toward the kitchen shed, the room fell quiet, except for the creaking of the fan. Doctor Hébert watched the black boy who crouched in the corner, pulling at the rope. His face was turned away toward the wall, and a large ear stuck out at right angles to his head.

"Restraint on the part of all factions is undoubtedly to be desired," Doctor Hébert said. He had accustomed himself to uttering such platitudes since he had first arrived in the colony. All political subjects were dangerously volatile, and he found it difficult to make a quick and accurate estimate of where anyone stood on them. He would have hesitated to express a sincere conviction even if he had had the opportunity of forming one.

"I should like to see the Pompons Rouge restrained with a weight of chains," Arnaud said. "That rabble at Port-au-Prince will ruin themselves as well as us if nothing is done to contain them. Though they do not know it. It is an appalling blindness. We got off easily from that affair of last October but I would not expect such a matter to go so fortunately a second time."

The slaves were now returning from the yard, carrying a silver coffee service and a platter of mango and lemon slices and another of small, dry cakes. Doctor Hébert accepted some pieces of fruit, tasted the mango, and sipped at his coffee.

"One might say that it went quite unfortunately for Ogé," he said.

"I am little concerned with Ogé's fortunes," Arnaud said. "He had done better to remain in France."

"Where many think it a hard punishment to be broken on a wheel of knives," the doctor said. "For a mulatto or for any man."

"Let it dissuade them from following his example, in that case," said Arnaud. "Ogé would have raised the cultivators. It is unthinkable."

"You speak freely," Doctor Hébert said, with an involuntary glance at the slave who stood behind Arnaud's chair, his face composed to a perfect blank.

"Free?" Arnaud said. "Sir, I have begun to develop a distaste for the sound of that word."

Above them, the fan creaked on its axis, wood fretting against wood. A film of sweat on the doctor's forehead was turning slightly chill. He moved his hand toward his wineglass, and the slave behind him leapt forward to refill it.

"You are lately come from France yourself?" Arnaud inquired.

"I have been here for about five weeks," the doctor said.

"And where were you bound when you came here?"

"From Ennery to Le Cap," Doctor Hébert said. "From Habitation Thibodet, near Ennery. The husband of my sister was the proprietor there."

"I do not know him."

"I believe you are fortunate," the doctor said. "He appears to have been seven parts scoundrel. The marriage was inadvisable—

by the result, at least. My sister had departed before I arrived and as yet I have been unable to trace her." He stopped speaking and cleared his throat, realizing that in his haste to avoid politics he had steered too deeply into personal confidences. He did not much care for the fruity smile on Arnaud's little mouth.

"And what of his other three parts, this Thibodet?"

"Oh, I would not deny him a degree of roguish charm, when he wished to exercise it. But he was three parts solid gold. I do not mean to be metaphorical. He was an extremely wealthy scoundrel."

"You employ the past tense."

"He died," Doctor Hébert said. "Quite suddenly, soon after my arrival at his house." He had not killed his brother-in-law, but there was that about Arnaud that made him wish it to appear as if he might have done so.

"It is an unhealthy country," Arnaud said. "Many die here."

"Yes," Doctor Hébert said. "I should mention that I am myself a doctor. And I would repay your hospitality—"

"We have no illness here," Arnaud said. "Though you are kind." He pushed his chair back, and the slaves again commenced to clear the table, as though his movement was a signal.

"And yourself?" Doctor Hébert said. "In what part of France did you originate?"

"I was born here," Arnaud said shortly, and stood up. "Excuse me." He picked up a candlestick and moved to a door behind his seat, which was shut with a padlock, and opened it with a key he took from his breeches pocket. From behind, his plumpness made him almost pear-shaped, and there was a hint of effeminacy in his step. The slave in the coat followed him into the room, where there must have been a draft, for the candle guttered. It was a storeroom, the doctor saw, with shelves of flour and other imported foods, many ranks of bottles, and more shelves of tools. Arnaud emerged with an axe in his hand. The slave came after him, carrying two mattocks.

"I have a little task outside," Arnaud said. "I will return momentarily."

"I believe I will accompany you," the doctor said.

Arnaud arched an eyebrow, but said nothing. The doctor followed him through the outer door. The slave who had waited on him at table now stood on the gallery with a lighted torch. At a word from Arnaud he led the way down the steps into the compound; Arnaud and the slave with the mattocks went after him. Doctor Hébert lagged a little way behind the procession. It was markedly cooler outside by this time. Though there was no moon, the sky was clear and so long as he kept away from the torchlight the stars were extraordinarily bright.

At the foot of the pole, Arnaud stopped and took the torch from the slave and raised it. From a few feet back, Doctor Hébert saw the woman's body illuminated as high as her rib cage. There was no evidence of breathing.

"Well, it is finished," Arnaud said. He spoke to the slaves in Creole, and they took up the mattocks and began digging at the base of the pole, which the doctor now saw was supported by a packing of rocks and earth. Arnaud watched the mattocks swinging. He set the axe head on the ground and leaned his weight on the handle. When the slaves had cleared the base of the pole, he smacked it with a one-handed swipe of the axe's blunt end. The two slaves sprang way as the pole fell backward. The woman's head bounced slackly against the wood, with a dense, compact sound. The pole rolled over a quarter turn and was stopped from rolling farther by her body.

Arnaud passed the torch back to the slave who had been holding it before and stood looking down at the corpse. He held the axe in both hands across his thighs in the same way he had earlier held his cane, the handle indenting his flesh slightly. The doctor stepped a little nearer to him.

"And what will become of the infant now?"

Arnaud snapped his head around. "How did you come to know about that?"

"My profession," the doctor said dryly, and pointed. "She had not even time to pass the afterbirth."

"Time?" Arnaud said. "She killed her child the moment it was born. She stole a nail and drove it through its head. *That* nail." He raised the axe high and struck down at the impaled hands, severing them both crisply at the wrists. The doctor was impressed by the force of the stroke.

"It was a child of the *Pariade*," Arnaud said. "Some sailor's bastard, a half-breed like your Ogé." He swung the axe again, and again. It took him four or five blows to cut through the ankles and he was breathing hard when he had done it.

"There," he said. "Let them raise that."

Doctor Hébert glanced at the two slaves, who stood as woodenly as they had behind the dinner table. "Do you really believe that they can raise the dead?"

"It is not a matter of what I believe." Head down, the axe angled out from Arnaud's hand, describing a pendulous arc over the dead woman's head. "I paid twelve hundred pounds for that, and not eight months ago. Breeding stock, if you like. It is ruinous. If not abortion, it is suicide. They are animals."

"One does not ordinarily torture animals," the doctor said. "I have never known an animal to be a suicide."

"You are a sentimentalist, perhaps," Arnaud said. "You believe they are like little children."

"I believe they are like men and women," Doctor Hébert said.

"Indeed," said Arnaud. "Then you must be a Jacobin."

"I consider myself to be a scientist," the doctor said.

Arnaud stared at him, then sighed. "You have lost your way," he said. "If you were going to Le Cap you have strayed considerably. There is a passable road from here to Marmelade and there you may rejoin the *grand chemin*."

"Thank you," the doctor said, looking back toward the *grand'case* and the small yellow squares of its candlelit windows. Behind the house the dog had recommenced to bark. "Well, I see that it is late. I had better retire."

"I am in a position to offer you a glass of brandy," Arnaud said.

"I think I had best decline," the doctor said. "I have had a long ride today and look forward to another tomorrow." He bowed and walked out of the circle of torchlight.

There was a glow from the crack beneath his bedroom door when he approached it, but he thought nothing of this; a slave had probably brought a candle while he had been in the yard. Head lowered, he sat down on a chair and dragged off his left boot, not looking up until something suddenly blocked the light. A woman stood between him and the candle, which glittered through the loose weave of her clothing and outlined every detail of her body in black. The doctor had not yet got used to the degree of undress Creole women affected. He stood up abruptly and stumbled forward on his unshod foot. The woman hooked her hands into the waistband of his breeches and sat down backward on the palliasse, drawing him down after her.

The doctor was obliged to brace his hands on her shoulders to keep his balance. The bare skin was a bluish white and hot to his touch. He had suspected some misguided extension of Arnaud's hospitality, sending a mulattress to his bed, but it was the same woman he had seen on the gallery when he arrived, Madame Arnaud, presumably. She had let her hair down; it hung in thin pale crinkles into the loosened throat of her negligee. Her face still had a prettiness about it, but was puffed out of shape, and the spots of high color at her cheekbones looked unnatural, though they were not paint. Her eyes were gray-green and the left pupil had shrunk smaller than the right because it was nearer to the candle. The eyes were pointed at Doctor Hébert but he would not have ventured to suppose what they really saw.

Removing her hands from his waistband felt like plucking the claws of a dead bird from a branch. He took a step backward, unsteady between his bare foot and his booted one.

"I am sorry to see that you are unwell," he said. "I do not think it very serious, however. An agitation of the nerves. You must rest for three hours in the heat of the day and of course take care to avoid the sun. Have your cook prepare a strong consommé each evening. Lemons and oranges are plentiful here; I would suggest that you partake of them often. It would be best to abstain from spiritous liquors for a time. Some wine, perhaps, to strengthen your blood. But for the moment, sleep will be your great restorer."

Madame Arnaud had gathered her hair and was holding it with one hand at the nape of her neck. A thin blue vein wriggled beneath the clear skin of her temple. Doctor Hébert recalled what her husband had said, *For a shot of rum, she would do no matter what.* However, it was common usage to keep the storeroom locked wherever there were so many house slaves. Also common usage for the mistress of the house to keep a key.

Madame Arnaud put her head to one side and smiled at him

with a queer jerk, the style of coquetry one might expect from a marionette on strings. The smile erased itself as quickly as it had appeared, and she rose and moved past him in short tripping steps and left the room. As she opened the door to depart, the doctor thought he might have seen Arnaud standing on the gallery, fidgeting with his cane. He shut the door after her and leaned on it with his palm. His head felt light and his stomach was uneasy and when he pulled his hands away he saw they had acquired a tremor. He undressed rapidly, hanging his garments one over another on the last peg on the wall. Kneeling beside the palliasse he crossed himself and said Our Father once hurriedly. At the rear of his mind the phrase repeated, *Oh let it not be fever.*

After the brief prayer he swung his legs up onto the bed and covered himself and lay there, concentrating on composure. The fevers here could cut a man down almost as quickly as the guillotine. The doctor breathed with care, deeply and deliberately, in and out. In a high corner of the room, shadows wavered over a spider web. When he reached to pinch out the candle, his hand had grown perfectly steady once more. But a little light still reached the room, over the partition walls, which stopped a few inches short of the ceiling. In the next room he could hear the sound of someone breathing. He lay in the half dark, rubbing the burnt tallow from the candle between his thumb and forefinger, thinking uselessly of one thing and another. Thibodet had seemed in perfect health the day he had arrived. After his affairs appeared a wretched tangle, despite the evidence of great wealth somewhere, or perhaps it was only because the doctor understood so little of plantation management. He did not much trust the *gérant,* who appeared to have partnered his brother-in-law in most of his debaucheries. Perhaps he, too, would die before long. In a week Thibodet had lost half his body weight and his skin had shrunk and yellowed on his skull and a black effluvia poured from his every orifice, soiling the bed faster than the slave could clean it. He lashed his head from side to side and cried that he had no notion where Elise might have gone, though he hoped she was at the devil. She had had as many lovers as he, he declared, and had probably eloped with one or another, to Jamaica or Martinique. She might have sailed in an American naval vessel, she might have run away to join the maroons. Thibodet bolted up and turned to vomit into a pan. The movement tumbled him out of the bed and the doctor felt himself spinning, too, delirious, as he saw her coming painfully toward him on the stumps of her ankles, arms outstretched. Madame Arnaud, or no, it was Elise herself, younger than she ought to have been, her face at sixteen, seventeen. Her gown was hanging off one shoulder. Blood spurted mightily from her severed wrists, and as she reached out to embrace her brother she opened her mouth and howled like a wolf. The doctor was on the floor beside the palliasse, bunched on his knees and knuckles, gasping and trembling. He shook himself and sat back on his heels. Now it was completely dark in the room, and a cool sweat bathed him. In the shed outside, the howling declined and broke off into that same deep-throated barking as before.

No, it was not fever, the doctor thought with a slight inward smile. Merely an agitation of the nerves. He got up and found his trousers on the peg and put them on. Barefoot and bare chested, he went out to the gallery. A breeze was shivering the cane mats that closed either end of the long porch. In the exhilaration of his escape from the nightmare, the doctor felt preternaturally sensitive; he could have counted the hairs on his chest when the breeze lifted them, or numbered the splinters on the post when he placed his palm against it. He was not leaning for support, but only caressing the wood.

Behind the house the dog stopped barking and he heard the scratching of its claws against the dirt as it began to run and then the muted smash of its body against the heavy door. There was something else. He went down the two steps from the gallery and started across the compound, toward the ragged line of trees that scattered away from the denser hedging of the entrance *allée*. His feet were tender; he could feel the powdered dust caking up between his toes, and whenever he stepped on a pebble he winced a little. By the time he had reached the trees his eyes had adjusted to the starlight. Beyond them the land dipped gently down and rose farther on and he could see one field after another checkered by the tight shrubbery of citrus trees that divided them, and he saw the starlight shining on the narrow channels that brought the water in. Where the cultivation ended, the land rose sharply up and up and was a mountain, and he could not have measured the height of it if not for the stippled patterns of stars that began to appear at its limit. That was where the drumming came from, one pattern so low he could not really hear it, only feel a dim vibration of the small bones in his ears, and another drum sounding higher, beaten intermittently, like a voice calling to someone and waiting for answer and calling again. Surely it would have waked any dreamer. The doctor's hands were curled over the prickly twigs of the two trees he had stopped between. His heart and lungs were working powerfully and there was a potent sense of health and vigor that seemed to rise through the soles of his bare feet and work through every vital part of him. He stood still there for quite a time and then began to circle around the edges of the compound.

The pole still lay where it had been, but every piece of the body had been removed and the nails also had been pulled out. Doctor Hébert stepped over it and walked back toward the *grand'case*. Arnaud was sitting on the gallery, dandling his cane, balancing it and letting it drop from the vertical and catching the ornate pommel just before it tilted out of his reach. The reddened point of his cheroot glowed and faded and swept down to his knee. The doctor wondered, as he came up, if he might have failed to notice his host there when he first left the house.

"You are wandering," Arnaud said. He rested the cane against his outstretched leg.

The doctor walked up the steps and stood beside him. "Something woke me," he said. "A silence. The dog stopped barking."

"That's how it is," Arnaud said. He held a bottle up to the doctor, who swallowed from it, tasting a grapy thickness of sticks and stems and then the brilliant heat of *eau-de-vie*.

"The dog," the doctor said. "That is an animal you have there. Do you always keep him penned?"

"It's necessary," Arnaud said. "I trained him for the *maréchaussée*. He only understands killing, this dog. There is a band of maroons in the area, very troublesome."

"There?" Doctor Hébert said, swinging his shoulders toward where the pitch-black of the mountain interrupted the spangled blue-black of the sky. The movement of the deeper drum still trembled at the limit of his hearing.

Arnaud pulled at his cheroot and flipped it over the edge of the board floor. It rolled a little way, sprinkling sparks, then stopped, the coal paling against the ground. Arnaud took the bottle from the doctor's hands and poured from it into the glass he held. "That may be," he said. "There will be slaves from this plantation, certainly. And from others which are near."

"Why do you not forbid such gatherings?" said the doctor.

"Oh, of course they are forbidden," Arnaud said, proffering the bottle. Doctor Hébert took it and held it out from the overhang of the roof so that it caught a glitter of the starlight. It was a slender, tapered vessel, the body just double the width of the elongated neck.

"They will be dancing," Arnaud said. "There are dances for the dead. One knows, even when one does not hear."

"Truly," Doctor Hébert said.

Arnaud swallowed noisily from his glass. "To them everything is forbidden," he said, "and to us everything is permitted. As you are a scientist, I leave it to you to determine the precise difference of our conditions."

"You surprise me," the doctor said, and took a last drink from the bottleneck. "Well, that will not be the work of a moment. I thank you again for everything." He set the bottle on the floor by Arnaud's chair and withdrew into the house.

The remainder of the night he slept without stirring, and woke automatically just at first light. He dressed quickly and quietly, lifted his saddlebags, and passed through the main room, which seemed dim and dingy at this hour. There was no sign of anyone stirring within. Outdoors the compound was also deserted, except for a pair of chickens picking gravel around the back, but the dog began barking when he passed its shed. The doctor's temples tightened at the sound.

In the stall the horse was nosing at the last scatter of a flake of hay. Doctor Hébert saddled and bridled it and gave it water at the trough. He had no appetite himself, and was eager to be gone. When the horse had drunk, he broke off another corner of sugar to give it. The horse took the sugar and then went on nuzzling and lipping the butt of his palm. The doctor curved his hand up to stroke the soft dark skin around its nostrils and spoke to the horse in gentle nonsense syllables. Thibodet had named it Espoir, which struck the doctor as somewhat ridiculous, considering that it was a gelding.

The dog broke off its barking sharply as Doctor Hébert led the horse outside and swung up into the saddle. He had scarcely had time to take note of the silence when he saw the chickens scatter and loft themselves into clumsy flight and the dog coming grimly between them, straight for him at a dead run. He yanked the horse in the direction of its leap and the dog struck the horse on its shoulder, sprawled back on the ground, and was up again instantly. The horse reared and let out a panicked whinny, wheeled, and bunched itself to kick. The doctor leaned down into the horse's mane and groped in the bottom of his right-hand saddlebag, blindly turning over his instruments and the sacks of medicines there. Again the dog was trying to close, and, turning the horse more tightly with his left hand, the doctor kicked out at it clumsily with his boot still in the stirrup. The dog's teeth clicked against the stirrup iron and it fell back and regrouped itself. Doctor Hébert straightened up in the saddle, bringing the pistol out of the saddlebag and bracing it over his left arm, which held the reins. When the dog launched itself he shot it once in its open mouth, and the bullet, exiting from the base of the skull, flipped it over backward. The dog lay thrashing on the packed ground and the doctor sighted at a place behind its ear and fired again. The dog convulsed and stretched its legs and the doctor felt confident that it was dead.

It seemed brighter and warmer than it had been and from all sides there was a jabbering in Creole. Several of the house slaves had come out of the different outbuildings and were edging in cautiously on the carcass of the dog, whose big splayed paws were still twitching in the dust. The horse was moving in nervous jerks and Doctor Hébert stroked its neck with the two free fingers of his left hand to calm it. His right hand still held the pistol pointing straight up. His ears were ringing from the shots and he felt giddy, as though the gunpowder smell had made him drunk. Arnaud had come out the back door of the *grand'case* and stood with his feet apart, looking from the doctor to the dog's body and back.

"Accept my apologies," Doctor Hébert said. "I had to give myself permission. You understand the predicament, I am sure."

Arnaud said nothing in reply, but merely went on looking. He was standing just as the doctor had first seen him when he had arrived the afternoon before, holding his cane in two hands and pressing it into the meat of his thighs. The doctor contemplated the curious thought that possibly everything which had occurred between the one stance and the other was an illusion and no time had really passed at all. He saluted Arnaud with the sulphurous barrel of the pistol, and kicked the horse and cantered around the corner of the house toward the mouth of the green *allée*.

CONTRIBUTORS' NOTES

Ploughshares · Winter 1993-94

MARGARET ATWOOD is the author of more than thirty books of poetry, fiction, and nonfiction. Her most recent novel, *The Robber Bride,* came out this fall from Doubleday. MADISON SMARTT BELL is the author of two collections of short stories—*Zero db* and *Barking Man*—and seven novels, including *Waiting for the End of the World, Soldier's Joy,* and, most recently, *Save Me, Joe Louis.* Since 1984, he has taught at Goucher College, where he is Writer-in-Residence. JAMES BLAND, a recipient of an Academy of American Poets Prize, is currently completing his doctorate at Harvard. His work has appeared or is forthcoming in *Callaloo, Key West Review, The Kenyon Review, Columbia Magazine, Agni,* and elsewhere. HAYDEN CARRUTH has published a total of twenty-eight books, chiefly of poetry, the latest of which are his *Collected Longer Poems* and *Suicides and Jazzers.* He has served as an editor at *Poetry, Harper's,* and *The Hudson Review,* and is the recipient of numerous fellowships and awards, including special recognitions from the Whiting Foundation, the National Book Critics' Circle, and the New York Foundation for the Arts. In 1988 he was appointed Senior Fellow by the National Endowment for the Arts. ROBERT CREELEY's edition of Charles Olson's *Selected Poems* was published recently by the University of California Press. His *Tales Out of School: Selected Interviews* and Tom Clark's *Robert Creeley and the Genius of the American Common Place* (which includes Creeley's "Autobiography") have just been released by, respectively, the University of Michigan Press and New Directions. FIELDING DAWSON is the author of nineteen books. An artist with the Jack Tilton Gallery in New York, as well as a critic, essayist, and lecturer, he is the chairman of the PEN Prison Writing Committee and periodically teaches at Attica, Sing Sing, and other prisons. DEBORAH DIGGES's first book of poems, *Vesper Sparrows,* won the Delmore Schwartz Memorial Poetry Prize in 1986. Her second collection, *Late in the Millennium,* was published in 1989 by Alfred A. Knopf. Earlier this year, her book of nonfiction, *Fugitive Spring,* was issued in paperback by Vintage. New poems which will be included in her third collection have recently appeared in *The Atlantic, The New Yorker, Antaeus,* and other magazines. She is an Assistant Professor of English at Tufts University. STEPHEN DOBYNS's eighth book of poems, *Velocities: New and Selected Poems, 1966-1992,* will be published by Viking Penguin in January 1994. His most recent novel, *The Wrestler's Cruel Study,* was published by W.W. Norton in August 1993. This coming summer, Norton will also publish Dobyns's eighth Saratoga mystery: *Saratoga Backtalk.* He directs the creative writing program at Syracuse University and teaches in the M.F.A. program at Warren Wilson College. JESSICA HAGEDORN is the author of the novel *Dogeaters,* which was nominated for a National Book Award, and of *Danger and*

Beauty, a collection of poetry and prose. She is the editor of *Charlie Chan Is Dead: An Anthology of Contemporary Asian American Fiction,* which has just been published by Viking Penguin. LOLA HASKINS's *Hunger* (Univ. of Iowa, 1993) won the 1992 Edwin Ford Piper Award. She has published four other books of poetry, most recently *Forty-Four Ambitions for the Piano* (Univ. of Florida, 1990). She lives on a farm outside Gainesville, Florida. GARRETT HONGO is the author of *Yellow Light* (Wesleyan, 1982) and *The River of Heaven* (Knopf, 1988), which was the Lamont Poetry Selection of the Academy of American Poets in 1987 and a finalist for the Pulitzer Prize in 1988. His poems and essays have appeared in *Antaeus, The American Poetry Review, Ploughshares,* and elsewhere. Recently, he edited *The Open Boat: Poems from Asian America* (Anchor, 1993) and *A New Perspective,* a special issue of *New England Review.* He is currently Director of Creative Writing at the University of Oregon. FANNY HOWE's most recent books are *Saving History,* a novel from Sun and Moon, and *The End,* a book of poems from Littoral Books. She lives in London. MARK JARMAN's most recent book is *Iris* (Story Line Press, 1992), a book-length narrative poem. His collection *The Black Riviera* (Wesleyan, 1990) won the Poet's Prize for 1991. David R. Godine will publish his next collection, *Questions for Ecclesiastes.* Jarman teaches at Vanderbilt University. LAURA KASISCHKE received the Elmer Holmes Bobst Award for Emerging Writers for her first collection of poems, *Wild Brides* (New York University Press, 1992). She also received the Poetry Society of America's Alice Fay DiCastagnola Award for a work-in-progress this year for her new collection, *Housekeeping in a Dream.* MARTIN LAMMON teaches writing and literature at Fairmont State College in West Virginia, where he also co-edits the new literary journal *Kestrel* and directs the Kestrel Writers Conference. His poems have recently appeared or are forthcoming in *The New Virginia Review, Mississippi Valley Review, Midwest Quarterly, West Branch,* and *The Gettysburg Review.* DANA LEVIN currently lives in New York City, where she is at work on her first book of poems, *Castle Perilous.* Her work appeared in the Spring 1992 issue of *Ploughshares.* ADRIAN C. LOUIS lives on the Great Plains of South Dakota. A new collection of his poems, *Blood Thirsty Savages* (Time Being Books), will be available in the spring of 1994. CLARENCE MAJOR is the author of nine books of poetry and seven novels, most recently *Painted Turtle: Woman With Guitar,* which was cited as a *New York Times Book Review* Notable Book of the Year in 1988. He regularly reviews books for *The Washington Post Book World* and has contributed to *The Kenyon Review, The American Poetry Review, Essence,* and numerous other periodicals and anthologies. He is currently directing the Creative Writing Program at the University of California, Davis. CLEOPATRA MATHIS has published three books of poems, the most recent of which is *The Center for Cold Weather.* She teaches at Dartmouth College. WILLIAM MATTHEWS's most recent book is *Selected Poems & Translations 1969-1991* (Houghton Mifflin). CAMPBELL MCGRATH is the author of *Capitalism* (Wesleyan) and the forthcoming *American Noise* (Ecco Press). His work has appeared in *The New Yorker, The New York Times, The Paris Review,* and *Antaeus.* He teaches at Florida International University in

Miami. PAUL MULDOON was born in 1951 in Northern Ireland. His most recent books are *Madoc: A Mystery* (1991) and *Selected Poems 1968-1986* (1993), both of which were published by Farrar, Straus and Giroux, and *Shining Brow* (1993), his libretto for an opera about Frank Lloyd Wright, which was issued by Faber and Faber. JOYCE CAROL OATES's latest novel is *Foxfire: Confessions of a Girl Gang*. She recently edited *The Oxford Book of American Short Stories*. ED OCHESTER's most recent collection of poetry is *Changing the Name to Ochester* (Carnegie Mellon). He is Director of the Writing Program at the University of Pittsburgh, editor of the Pitt Poetry Series, and, with Peter Oresick, editor of *The Pittsburgh Book of Contemporary American Poetry*. SHARON OLDS teaches at New York University and at the university's writing workshop at Goldwater Hospital, which serves the severely disabled. The workshop, now in its seventh year, will be Olds's community project for her 1993-96 Lila Wallace–Reader's Digest Fund Fellowship. Her most recent book is *The Father* (Knopf, 1992). STANLEY PLUMLY's last book is *Boy on the Step* (Ecco, 1989). He is a Professor of English at the University of Maryland. THOMAS RABBITT lives and works on a farm in Elrod, Alabama. His fourth book of poems, *Enemies of the State*, is due from David R. Godine, Publisher, in early 1994. JAN RICHMAN's poetry has appeared in *The Nation, Caliban, Grand Street, The Bloomsbury Review*, and elsewhere. In 1993, she received a "Discovery"/*The Nation* Award and the Celia B. Wagner Award from the Poetry Society of America. She is currently at work on a novel. LEON ROOKE has published thirteen short story collections. His novels include *A Good Baby* (Knopf and Vintage) and *Shakespeare's Dog* (Knopf and Ecco). Earlier this fall, he was Writer-in-Residence at Intersection for the Arts in San Francisco. He lives in Canada. KENNETH ROSEN lives in Portland, Maine, and teaches at the University of Southern Maine. Recent poems have appeared in *The Massachusetts Review* and *The Paris Review*. His collections of poems include *Whole Horse* (Braziller), which was nominated for the Pulitzer Prize, and *The Hebrew Lion* and *Longfellow Square*, both from the Ascensius Press. NATASHA SAJE's poems have recently appeared or are forthcoming in *The Gettysburg Review, Poetry, Feminist Studies, The Virginia Quarterly Review*, and elsewhere. REG SANER's book of nonfiction, *The Four-Cornered Falcon: Essays on the Interior West and the Natural Scene*, appeared this spring from Johns Hopkins. He teaches at the University of Colorado, Boulder. TIM SEIBLES is the author of two books of poetry, *Body Moves* (Corona Press, 1988) and *Hurdy-Gurdy* (Cleveland State, 1992). An NEA Fellow in 1990, he recently received the Open Voice Award for poetry from the National Writers' Voice Project at New York's West Side YMCA. He is the Writing Coordinator at the Fine Arts Center in Provincetown, Massachusetts. JAN SELVING is an M.F.A. candidate at Arizona State University in Tempe. Her poems have been published or will appear in *Denver Quarterly, The Antioch Review,* and *The Jazz Poetry Anthology*. LAURIE SHECK is the author of *Io at Night* (Knopf, 1990). She was a Guggenheim Fellow in Poetry in 1991, and has had recent work in *The New Yorker, The Paris Review,* and *Michigan Quarterly Review*. She teaches as Rutgers University. SUSAN SNIVELY's books are *From This Distance* (Alice James Books, 1981) and *Voices in the House* (Univ. of Alabama, 1988). Her new manuscript is *The Speed of the Drift.* She lives in Amherst, Massachusetts. **DANNYKA TAYLOR** lives in the Pacific Northwest. **MELANIE RAE THON** is the author of two novels, *Iona Moon* (Poseidon, 1993) and *Meteors in August* (Random House, 1990), and a collection of stories, *Girls in the Grass* (Random House, 1991). Originally from Montana, she currently teaches in the Graduate Writing Program at Syracuse University. **BRUCE WEIGL** is the author of six poetry collections, most recently *What Saves Us* (TriQuarterly Books, 1992), and the editor of the forthcoming *The Phenomenology of Spirit and Self: On the Poetry of Charles Simic* (Story Line Press). In 1994, the University of Massachusetts Press will publish *Poems from Captured Documents,* which he translated from the Vietnamese with Nguyen Thanh. Weigl teaches in the writing program at Pennsylvania State University. **MARIANNE WIGGINS**'s books include *John Dollar, Bet They'll Miss Us When We're Gone,* and *Separate Checks.* She lives and writes in New York City, where she rides the M5 bus. **DEAN YOUNG** has published two books of poems, *Design with X* (1988) and *Beloved Infidel* (1992), both from Wesleyan. He teaches at Loyola University in Chicago.

ABOUT RUSSELL BANKS

Ploughshares · Winter 1993-94

*C*ontinental Drift, Russell Banks's fifth novel, begins with an invocation: *"It's not memory you need for telling this story... it's clear-eyed pity and hot, old-time anger and a Northern man's love of the sun, it's a white Christian man's entwined obsession with race and sex and a proper middle-class American's shame for his nation's history."* The passage says as much about Russell Banks as it does about Bob Dubois, the central character of the book. Within those brief lines are adumbrations of Banks's concerns as a writer and as a citizen, of his mastery at turning words into incantations, his urgency as a storyteller, his personal roots and demons.

Like Dubois, Russell Banks grew up in the working-class environs of the Northeast. Born in 1940 in Newton, Massachusetts, he was raised in New Hampshire—principally in the town of Barnstead—until he was twelve. His parents then moved Banks, his sister, and his two brothers to Wakefield, Massachusetts, and divorced shortly thereafter. Banks has been candid about the physical abuse he suffered under the hands of his father, Earl, an alcoholic plumber. As a two-year-old, Banks lost the mobility of his left eye, an impairment he attributes to a blow from Earl, although his mother always claimed—somewhat improbably—that it was due to whooping cough. Banks would spend a good deal of his adult life trying to reconcile his relationship with his father, but at the time, he exhibited few emotional scars (they would come later, in his twenties, manifested by a pervasive rage, heavy drinking, and barroom brawls).

Other than being self-conscious about looking cross-eyed, Banks says he was a pretty normal teenager, playing sports and doing well academically. Indeed, he was so precocious and quick-witted, he was given the nickname "Teacher," and Colgate University offered him a full scholarship. With a vague fantasy of becoming a lawyer, he left for the all-white, all-male school in 1958, the first in his family to attend college.

Once there, however, Banks was overwhelmed. Colgate was then a bastion for the sons of captains of industry, and Banks immediately felt inadequate and out of place. After eight weeks, he quit. "It was a terrible failure, a cloud of shame," Banks says. "I converted that, as one often converts shame when it feels intolerable, into a political romance." That winter, Fidel Castro was in the mountains above Havana, and the American media was portraying the guerrilla leader as a hero. Banks took off to join Castro, hitchhiking down to Florida, a flight impassioned further by Jack Kerouac's *On the Road*. The book justified the trip on "religious, metaphysical, social, and political terms," Banks remembers. "Kerouac was a working-class boy from Lowell, and it wasn't too hard to make an identification."

Banks got as far as St. Petersburg, where he ran out of money, and then spent the next two years shuffling around Florida. He married and had the first of his four daughters, worked odd jobs, and started thinking of himself as an artist. Always gifted in drawing and painting, he began dabbling with poetry and stories as well. He admits he was inspired as much by the lifestyle as anything else: "Bohemianism is a useful way for a person to drop out of the class wars of America."

When his marriage ended, Banks moved back north, to Boston. He befriended other writers, musicians, and beatniks living in the Back Bay, but he was soon broke. Growing more serious and disciplined about his writing, he sought an alternative to his itinerant bohemianism. He returned to New Hampshire, where his father helped him get a union card and jobs as a pipe fitter and plumber. Father and son achieved a level of rapprochement, and Banks "was happy working alongside him and living in some degree the kind of life that he had," but their relationship was still tense, and it took many more years for them to accept each other fully. "It was always easy for him to turn his back and be passive about relations," Banks reflects. "You almost had to force yourself on him, but in the end I think it was a good thing for him as well, because we ended up loving each other very, very much."

In 1964, Banks enrolled as a student at the University of North Carolina at Chapel Hill, an opportunity provided by his second wife's mother, who offered to pay the tuition. After years of self-

PHOTO: NATHAN FARB

teaching, he reveled in the stimulation of being in an academically structured environment, and he found literary compatriots in the poet William Matthews and a group of others, with whom he established a new journal and press called Lillabulero, after a failed attempt to usurp *The Carolina Quarterly*. In addition, the civil rights movement was burgeoning, and Banks participated in organized political activity for the first time. "It wasn't really until Chapel Hill that race became a meaningful part of my sense of self and sense of American history," he says. "It was an important kind of awakening."

After graduating Phi Beta Kappa, Banks took a teaching job at Emerson College for two years, then accepted a post at the University of New Hampshire at Durham. Meanwhile, he was writing at a prolific rate. His stories began appearing in respectable journals such as *New American Review, Antaeus,* and *The Partisan Review,* and in the space of seven years, he published three volumes of poetry, three story collections, and four novels. The reaction to his work was mixed. Even Banks is bemused when thinking of his initial efforts at poetry: "Everybody has his apprentice work or juvenilia, and the trouble with being a writer is that you sort of have to grow up in public. I cringe a little over some of the early poems, and I make every attempt I can to destroy those when I come across them."

But more frustratingly, Banks was not given sufficient credit for the extraordinary range and innovation of his fiction during this period. Readers and critics were often perplexed by his experimental novels, which frequently put historical characters in contemporary contexts and employed a rococo style, freely shifting points of view and breaking all narrative conventions. Interspersed were books with the social realism and naturalistic language for which Banks would become famous—melancholy stories set in New Hampshire and the tropics, exploring the pain and loneliness of the poor; the polarities of good and evil; class struggles in which the disenfranchised become both perpetrators and victims of violence. Even today, after three more or less traditional novels in a row (*Continental Drift, Affliction,* and *The Sweet Hereafter*), Banks does not dismiss the possibility of returning to more metafictional projects. "People expect each book to grow out of the previous book, sort of like a plant exfoliating," he says. "But choosing between these modes of writing is, for me, not a profound aesthetic choice. It's really a matter of using one way of writing to get to what you need to say. Looking back, I can see I wrote that kind of fiction—formalistic, allegorical, sometimes satirical—when I was most angry and disoriented. I reached for high artifice in times of disarray, and I turned to more conventionally realistic fiction when I was most affectionate toward the world, and felt anchored and solid in my life. But who's to say I won't again feel as angry as I felt when I wrote *Family Life* or *The Relation of My Imprisonment* or *Hamilton Stark*?"

For the moment, however, Banks seems content. After teaching at New England College, Sarah Lawrence, NYU, the University of Alabama, and Columbia, he found a home in 1982 at Princeton University, where he is a tenured full professor. *Continental Drift*, which was published in 1985, was considered a critical and commercial breakthrough, and ever since, his place among the first rank of writers in this country has been assured. He has earned a devout readership and numerous honors—including the John Dos Passos Award, an American Academy of Arts and Letters Award, an American Book Award, and runner-up nominations for the Pulitzer Prize and PEN/Faulkner—and by and large, he has secured the comfortable lifestyle of a working writer. Currently he is at Princeton only one semester a year, and he and his fourth wife, the poet Chase Twichell, spend most of their time at a house in the Adirondacks.

Banks works in a converted sugarhouse in the woods, writing every morning, alternating between longhand and a computer to draft out at least three pages a day. He is in the middle of a historical novel about John Brown, a mid-1800s abolitionist, and a contemporary novel about a fourteen-year-old mall rat. Disparate as they seem, the books are bound by vintage Banks themes of alienation and rebellion. He doesn't believe American civilization has evolved very much since Brown's time. "I don't think we're facing an apocalypse," he says, "but I'm beginning to fear that we are facing the death of our culture, and the atomization of human beings in it. And I think one of the quests of my own work is to identify the possibilities of resistance to that atomization."

Yet, while no one would suggest that Banks has tempered the iconoclastic bent of his fiction or politics, it's obvious from the patience and good humor he exudes that he is very much at peace with his personal life. "Over the years, I think that I've been able to make my anger coherent to myself," he says, "and that's allowed me to become more lucid as a human being, as a writer, as—I hope—a husband, father, and friend. It's very hard to be a decent human being if you're controlled by anger that you can't understand. When you begin to acquire that understanding, you begin to become useful to other people."

This redemptive notion—that coherence leads to humanity—is what sustains Russell Banks. He writes in the envoi of *Continental Drift*: "*Good cheer and mournfulness over lives other than our own, even wholly invented lives—no, especially wholly invented lives—deprive the world as it is of some of the greed it needs to continue to be itself. Sabotage and subversion, then, are this book's objectives. Go, my book, and help destroy the world as it is.*"

—*Don Lee*

ABOUT CHASE TWICHELL

Ploughshares · Winter 1993-94

Chase Twichell grew up in two geographies: One was New Haven, Connecticut, which she says had little effect on her, except perhaps to put the second in relief. The other was Keene, New York, in the heart of the high hills of the Adirondacks, "a rocky, rough, mountains-and-valleys, fast cold water, lakes-in-the-middle-of-nowhere place" her family had visited for generations and where she still spends over half her time. "Everyone thinks it's pretty when they first drive through," she says, "but my father says really it's a virus that gets you, and then you have to be near it or you die." Her infection appears serious: the place itself seems her inspiration, a touchstone not only for her poetry but for her perspective of the world. Perhaps, though, New Haven, where her father taught Latin and coached baseball at nearby Choate, a prep school, has had more effect than Twichell lets on; her poetry marries an urbane intellectual rigor—a classical grace and distance—to the passion of one who loves the world outside the window.

Although both her father and mother were literary and Twichell was reading poetry early on ("At twelve, I loved Yeats; of course it was the bad Yeats—all that Celtic twilight, broken hearts, and so forth"), painting was her first love. She was so fanatical about it, her parents feared she was becoming "socially abnormal." When she left for boarding school at thirteen, her parents and the school conspired to forbid her to take any art classes. "That's when I started writing poetry. I did it for revenge." Since then, she has received several prestigious awards and grants, published three books of poetry (*Northern Spy, The Odds,* and *Perdido*), finished a fourth, and co-edited *The Practice of Poetry.*

After graduating from Trinity College in Hartford, Twichell, who now teaches at Princeton, went to the Iowa Writers' Workshop, a choice determined by the opportunity to minor in typography and design there. While in Iowa, she apprenticed at Windhover Press for a year, and after receiving her M.F.A., she worked with illustra-

PHOTO: ARTURO PATTEN

tor Barry Moser for nine years at Pennyroyal Press in western Massachusetts. "I taught when I was in grad school," she says, "and it was what I always thought I would do, but I was appalled at how much of the energy I needed for writing it stole.... I was worried that I wasn't going to be able to teach and write in the same life, so I opted for manual labor, and it was great. I loved it." The time came, however, when she felt she should either start her own press or move on to something else. She found, after accepting a job at the University of Alabama, that in the decade between graduate school and teaching she had "acquired the discipline—well, maybe not the discipline but the habit—of writing. I guess, too, I felt established enough as a writer to feel that teaching was not a threat to it." Teaching led Twichell to the idea for *The Practice of Poetry,* a collection of writing exercises from more than eighty poets, which she co-edited with Robin Behn and which is becoming a standard workshop text.

Around the same time, she says she had to "pull my head out of the apolitical sand," placing the environment at the top of her list of causes. Whereas her third book, *Perdido,* addresses individual mortality, the book she has just finished, *The Ghost of Eden,* is the record of her confrontation with what she calls "Earth mortality."

"I think our planet is endangered, not just because of the ozone and the rain forest, but because it seems that the human relation to nature has been changed forever in only the last ten or twenty years, and that this is of such profound significance we can hardly begin to understand it. I grew up in nature. It's been my solace and my teacher forever, and I see it dying around me. Looking out the window, I see that the beeches and the red spruces and the birches are all suffering heavily from acid rain. All the birch leaves have little blisters on them and discolored spots; there's a beech blight; the maples are threatened; they're all in stress, and I can't help but see all the things going wrong. I can't just say, 'Oh, isn't it a pretty day.' I look out the window and say, 'Oh, isn't it a pretty day. Look at those maples dying.'"

She had expected the book to follow the conventional form of mourning, that in the end she would feel more remote than at the height of grief, the way one sometimes does when a loved person dies, but she discovered something else: it was the world itself that was absent, making one's presence in it the painful thing. The title, *The Ghost of Eden,* is a pun: "The ghost of Eden is the remnant world, on one hand," she says, "but the real ghost turns out to be me. I'm the one who's wandering around weightless, and that made fighting through these poems emotionally and intellectually difficult. But now that I've done it, there's another surprise, which is that there is a heightening effect where everything becomes more beautiful and valuable. Death is the counterweight, the same old theme.

"I probably shouldn't confess such things in public," Twichell says, "but I think about it at least ten times a day." Contrary to what one might assume, her obsession has given her tremendous vitality and the ability to laugh easily and often. "It's not all about tears and sadness and grief," she says. "It becomes funny; it becomes interesting."

One day, she and her husband, the novelist Russell Banks, decided to get a cemetery plot. "In the town of Keene, a plot for two in this beautiful cemetery up on a hill, with views of the mountains in both directions, sixteen by twenty-four feet, cost us one hundred dollars. We even got a little deed and everything. Michael Harper was visiting us one day, and we took him up there to see our new piece of real estate, our future home. There's something about being able to goof about it like that that makes it part of the continuum, that's not alien, and, I guess, that makes me feel less terrorized by world death and person death."

Twichell has melded her divided geographies—both physical and psychic—allowing her to bring the forcefulness and élan that have always been present in her poetry into her politics. She writes lots of crank letters to corporations, tells people to boycott L'Oréal for testing suntan lotion on mice, packs up a box full of catalogues from Barnes and Noble that continue to arrive, fifty a month, despite letters and calls, and returns them. "I sent them to the customer service manager," she laughs, "but I never heard a word, and I'm still getting catalogues, so I'm going to have to get even more radical."

—David Daniel

BOOKSHELF

THE VERY AIR *A novel by Douglas Bauer. William Morrow, $20.00 cloth. Reviewed by Alexandra Marshall.*

In *The Very Air,* Douglas Bauer's second novel, "Doctor" Luther Mathias builds an empire with his pirate radio station, which broadcasts illegally over the border into the U.S. in the early part of this century. As events conspire to undo him, he crazily makes a last-ditch transmission and exhorts his "brave and independent-thinking listeners" to write to their elected officials and pressure "the feckless boobs" of the Federal Communications Commission, those "spineless commissioners who don't have the courage to think for themselves and yet who would presume to legislate the ether! Who act as if they own the very air!"

This is a novel about multiple woes and nearly successful cures, with a genius-rogue of a protagonist hanging in the balance. Luther Mathias is instructed early in life by a role-model uncle that "Another reason this country is great is that if the history you've been handed doesn't suit your purpose, you're free to proceed and get another one....I believe it's openly implied in our U.S. Constitution." But Uncle Ray White has only a primitive sense of the potential of his own modest placebo compound, and it takes Luther to go on to devise the ultimate: "a prosaic cure for an imaginative ailment," which involves pretending to perform gonad-replacement surgery as a cure to "the unspeakable sadness of sexual weakness."

Of course, you may think this isn't funny, or this isn't your kind of guy, or this is exactly what's *wrong* with our country. Who needs to sympathize, you might well think, with such a desperate faker, such a manipulator? And you might have a point, in fact, which might be why Douglas Bauer doesn't just drop you into the middle of the listening audience like one more innocent victim. Instead, he does the humane thing, which is to begin nearer the beginning, so you can experience not just the how but the why of Luther Mathias.

At this, Douglas Bauer displays a remarkable proficiency with character development. He enables the reader to understand character formation in a way that then enables compassion, even for such a man as Luther, even by the hardest-hearted among us. Luther Mathias lives on each page and demands to be taken seriously. As he will be. As he already is.

The text is also enlivened by the sheerly acrobatic mind of this master schemer, "a poet of a thrillingly severe language of pseudo-medicine." But perhaps more importantly, the narrator's voice is gifted, too, with such a sensibility as to be able to notice "a misrepresentative meanness" in the face of Luther's mother, a young woman aged "from the strain of her life on a tiny livestock farm five miles from Cliffside, Texas." This narrative voice is often critical, looking back as it does from our time to the earliest decades of this century, but it is also, importantly, empathetic.

The Very Air tells an important story of what we in our age have come to call consumer fraud, but it is for a better reason than this that it comes to you highly recommended. As a novel, it works to suspend not only disbelief, but disregard. Luther Mathias takes his history, like it or not, and freely proceeds and gets another one. As Uncle Ray White has taught him, he believes this right is openly implied in the very U.S. Constitution.

Alexandra Marshall, the author of three novels and a nonfiction book, is Co-Director of the Ploughshares International Fiction Writing Seminar at Castle Well in the Netherlands.

DEVOLUTION OF THE NUDE *Poems by Lynne McMahon. David R. Godine, Publisher, $12.95 paper. Reviewed by David Daniel.*

The best works in Lynne McMahon's *Devolution of the Nude* seem like found poems, unlikely jewels turned up in some nearby but rarely visited garden of the mind. The freshness of her language provides both delight and terror in the book, which reveals as it obscures, and obscures as it reveals, inviting the reader to enter with humility and humor into the heart of things.

McMahon's poems stop and start, tantalize, dangle on the verge of giving or taking away; they have the quality of an extraordinary conversation with one's spirit, revising, growing, transforming the overwhelming stuff of life into a comprehensible, if not comfortable, vision. In "Artifact," a pacifier is discovered "lint-wrapped from its long hiding" and becomes the center of a meditation on substitution, our disaffection from the "unalterable form." The poem moves gracefully and wittily from this almost comic solemnity to the searing deadpan of "And arcing between all such masculine histories / the curved simulacrum of the breast, shape of the planet, / some have said, the Eternal Feminine— / or would be, if these new age pacifiers were not / so bulbous / at their tip, so elongated at the shaft."

"Hopkins and Whitman" reveals as much about the book's strategy—and is as beautiful—as any poem in the collection. First stating "Hard to imagine two men more unlike," McMahon goes on to show how they were also similar: "How magnetic the expanse / between fastidious and crude when cast / into the field of dappled things!" One feels these poets' presence in several of the poems; in "Barbie's Ferrari," where Barbie and her Ferrari show perhaps Whitman at one pole of the magnet, Hopkins, in the last lines, stands at the other: "It's the car she was born for. / It's Barbie you mourn for." The result of this sort of juxtaposition throughout the book is the paradoxical creation of a continuum, which allows escape from the trap of nostalgia without sacrificing historical perspective. The resulting poems are startlingly present, alive, and original.

CHILD IN AMBER *Poems by Stephen McNally. University of Massachusetts Press, $20.00 cloth. Reviewed by Peter Jay Shippy.*
Tomaž Šalamun wrote that every true poet is a monster. If so, perhaps it is because monsters slap us into a sweet apoplexy from which we can't escape ourselves. The poems in Stephen McNally's Juniper Prize–winning first collection speak "with the unwavering clarity / of a hysterical child" ("Their Voices"), wondrously lost in worlds "without homes, without desire for them" ("The Final Despair"). It is our good magic that McNally's travelers—his *voyants* in the Symbolist sense—are never at a loss for language. And while some poems knowingly nod to Desnos, Cavafy, and Vallejo, they are at all times American poems about the democratic decay of the American century.

McNally's dispossessed speakers see their futures in a diner's meat loaf special; they are accosted by the insane in post offices; they visit the spots where children died; they transform TV test patterns into oracles. As the conquistador narrator of "Report From the Interior" says, "Anyone looking at us might say we're madmen just released, / or a group of religious fanatics sent out on a goose chase by a trickster god / who dresses us in bright armor." And what happens when there are no arms to discover or conquer? McNally looks inward for buried treasures or often up at beautiful, yet oblique, fields of stars. His people get into their cars and drive for the sake of movement—terrified that even as the creep of existence is catalogued, the miracle just slipped by. The speaker of "There's Really No Reason I Should Worry, Since There's No Way of Knowing What's Really Going On" says, "The day Jesus comes back I'll / be at the grocery store bending over meat..."

Child in Amber shows us that while the mysteries of existence may be beyond rational explanation, gods are in the grammar of trying. McNally is a brave and excellent guide. In "Sentenced," he writes, "my front door was the entrance to Hell. / But I went inside anyway." His monsters descend so we can, if not ascend, at least hover.

Peter Jay Shippy's work has appeared in Ploughshares, The Denver Quarterly, Epoch, *and elsewhere. He teaches at Emerson College.*

CAMELLIA STREET *A novel by Mercè Rodoreda, translated by David H. Rosenthal. Graywolf Press, $20.00 cloth. Reviewed by James Carroll.*

"They abandoned me on Camellia Street, in front of a garden gate, and the night watchman found me early the next morning."

So begins *Camellia Street,* a small masterpiece of fiction by Mercè Rodoreda, the Catalan novelist who died of cancer a decade ago. *Camellia Street* was first published in 1966 in the Catalan language. This new Graywolf edition, exquisitely translated by David H. Rosenthal, should introduce American readers to this important writer's work and, for that matter, to its meaning in the context of Catalan politics.

Rodoreda was one of many noted writers and artists driven from Spain after the defeat of the Republic in 1939. Her language was suppressed by Franco. Carol Gilligan writes of the voicelessness against which women struggle, but here was a woman for whom voicelessness was compounded by languagelessness. She published nothing for twenty years. But then in 1959 her stories and novels began to appear again. In Rodoreda, the silenced Catalan people—especially women—found a voice. *Camellia Street,* a simple, stark story about one woman's struggle on the streets of Barcelona, was read as a manifesto of resistance and survival. When Mercè Rodoreda returned to her homeland in 1979, it was as a literary hero.

As the opening sentence implies, *Camellia Street* is about the effect on a life of beginning as one abandoned. Cecilia C., as she is called, grows up to be a grotto-eyed streetwalker, then a wily kept woman who learns to use the men who use her. Her surfaces become as hard as her secret longing is pointed. She is forever at the mercy of a desire she cannot name.

Referring to the statues she collects, Cecilia says, "I kept buying angels and having them delivered to my house. I had tall and short ones, with curls and straight hair, with goblets, palm branches and grapes in their hands. . . . But they were silent, stiff, worm-eaten, earth-bound."

"I fell in love with the wall facing my bed," Cecilia says another time. And in answer to her long-lost foster father's question, "What have you done with your life," Cecilia muses, "I was about to tell him I'd spent it searching for lost things and burying dead loves, but I didn't say anything, and acted like I hadn't heard him."

Rodoreda's novel is written in the form of Cecilia's utterly unembellished, completely convincing stream of consciousness. The wall between the reader and what's read—between oneself and Cecilia—falls away, and it is only on reflection that the full achievement of this novel can be grasped. The work renders, first, the feeling of a woman abandoned by her parents, her lovers, and her miscarried children; second, it renders the plight of a people abandoned by the century; and third, most magnificently, it renders the basic experience of every human being—that we are all here on the earth as abandoned ones, that our lives are a long and futile search for "lost things."

In the face of the essential agony of the human condition, our books tell us, we can do only one of two things: offer the feeling up in prayer, or tell stories about it. Mercè Rodoreda, with *Camellia Street*, reminds us that even if prayer seems to have failed, stories have not.

James Carroll is the author of eight novels, most recently Memorial Bridge. *His new novel,* The City Below, *will be published in April 1994 by Houghton Mifflin. He teaches writing at Emerson College.*

STAINED GLASS *Poems by Rosanna Warren. W.W. Norton, $17.95 cloth. Reviewed by Jonathan Aaron.*

In "Tide Pickers," one of the tough-minded, beautifully crafted meditations in Rosanna Warren's third collection of poems, the speaker sees the figures of people digging for shellfish on the Brittany coast as "Question marks at the tide line." She wonders of the ocean, *"will it feed us?,"* a question that leads, with the disturbing logic that characterizes many of the poems in this book, to *"how will we / die?"* Her pondering ends with the onset of dusk "as Venus rises" and as, "framed in the window, a man and a woman bend / down into each other, carving that question / the sea won't answer though human hand grasp hand." Even at its most benign, Nature is both indifferent and inscrutable, prompting questions about our relation to it—our role in it—that are unanswerable. The lovers' embrace suggests one way people try to brace themselves against the knowledge the poem's speaker seems to be contending with. But "framed" here offers ironically disparate meanings—to build, to put into words, but also to incriminate falsely. The word's shiftiness subtly undercuts the solace that might be inferred from the image of the lovers. Bending "into" each other, they seem unaware of what the poem gently but somberly insists on—that a sense of life's meaning is momentary, that even love can offer little to offset whatever "evening" in this case will darken into.

Stained Glass is a book about endings. It starts with "Season Due," a terse yet richly visual contemplation of September's "chrysanthemums, brash / marigolds, fat sultan dahlias a-nod // in rain." The season's last, they "brazen out this chill / which has felled already gentler flowers and herbs // and now probes / these veins for a last / mortal volley of // cadmium orange, magenta, a last acrid flood / of perfume that will drift in the air here once more, / yet once more, when these stubborn flowers have died." In the poems that follow, Warren goes on to explore other kinds of endings, or limits that point to endings. One begins, "Once you have described the barn, erase the page" and ends as "Mist deletes the horizon" ("Farm"). A deft translation of Reverdy sounds a similar note: "The wind rises / The world slips away / The other side" ("Verso"). An electrifying rendering of Max Jacob's comic, finally visionary monologue "Christ at the Movies" momentarily suggests that endings sometimes lead to spiritual renewal: "Then why? Why this grace / If you know my life in all its ugliness? / If you know my faults and my weaknesses too? / What in me, oh Lord, could interest you?" The power of "grace," however, seems undermined by the sense of unworthiness and doubt revealed in the closing question.

Some of the book's starkest, boldest moments occur in poems on the death of Warren's father, on her mother's consequent solitude, and on the near loss of her own daughter. These poems are also among Warren's loveliest, as when, addressing her dying father, she sees "Your skin / as fragile, pale, and infinitesimally moist / as erasable bond; your look, a startled bound / of apprehension, subsiding / into its lair" and then wonders "What intersections can we appoint / between your knowledge / and ours?" ("His Long Home"). In these instances, her language honed to a sometimes eerie purity of image and diction, Warren's consciousness seems stripped down (or raised) to the point where she's capable of perceiving only essentials. Her concluding poem, "The Twelfth Day," breaks out of elegy and away from the personal by suddenly, shockingly recalling Achilles's treatment of Hector's corpse in *The Iliad*, 22: "...Achilles hoards and defiles the dead / So what if heaven // and earth reverberate / *release*... // ... // So what if everything / echoes the Father *let go let / go* This is Ancient // Poetry It's supposed / to repeat / ... / It's formulaic / That's how we love It's called // compulsion...." This daring stroke of self-deflation throws into a different kind of question all of the book's preceding poems. It's a grimly sardonic, finally almost unbearable gesture of refusal.

In Warren's view, the consolation of either elegy *or* philosophy is insufficient, and she's not going to let either herself or her reader forget it. *Stained Glass* is a work of acute, uncompromising vision.

Jonathan Aaron's most recent book of poetry is Corridor *(Wesleyan–New England). He teaches at Emerson College.*

Miscellaneous Notes · Winter 1993-94

ZACHARIS AWARD *Ploughshares* and Emerson College are proud to announce that Jessica Treadway has been named the 1993 recipient of the John C. Zacharis First Book Award for her short story collection, *Absent Without Leave and Other Stories.* The annual $1,500 award—which is sponsored by Emerson College and named after its former president, John C. Zacharis—honors the best debut book of short fiction or poetry published by a *Ploughshares* writer.

Treadway was born in 1961 in Albany, New York. She studied English literature and journalism at the State University of New York at Albany, and upon graduation, worked as a news and feature reporter for United Press International in Rochester. In 1984, after she published her first short story in *The Hudson Review,* she decided to concentrate on her fiction writing and moved to Boston. Subsequently, her short stories appeared in *The Atlantic Monthly, Ploughshares,* and *The Agni Review.* To support her writing endeavors during these years, she took part-time jobs as a baby-sitter, waitress, bookseller, legal secretary, and teacher.

Treadway credits her five-year participation in a writers' group led by Andre Dubus for her growth as a writer, but she says what has also sustained her is an absolute certainty that fiction writing is her calling, that it is a passion she cannot relinquish. She wrote her first story when she was four years old, and she can still recite it in its entirety: "Johnny likes to climb trees. He fell out of a tree and broke his leg. He ran into the house to tell his mother. His mother put a Band-Aid on his leg. The end." She remembers showing the story to her mother, who was encouraging, but asked, very seriously, "Honey, do you think if he broke his leg, he could run into the house?" Treadway recounts, "I'll never forget that moment of realizing that this wasn't going to be as easy as just saying that something happened. It was my first confrontation with plot."

In 1993, Treadway's collection, *Absent Without Leave and Other Stories,* was published by Delphinium Books/Simon & Schuster to enthusiastic praise: "A deft debut," said *Kirkus Reviews.* "This powerful, unforgettable collection of ten short stories will mesmerize the reader...highly recommended," wrote *Library Journal.* "Treadway's stories reveal a writer with an unsparing bent for the truth," noted *The New York Times Book Review.* And it's clear that the book found an audience as well: the entire printing sold out in less than six months (publishers interested in paperback rights should contact Delphinium Books at 212-362-1104).

The stories in *Absent Without Leave* are emotionally raw, unflinching in their honesty and generous in their depth. Many of the characters in the book succumb to their weaknesses—frequently to alcoholism—in the absence of consolation, and Treadway is able to render the tragic and cruel things people do to each other with authority and compassion. Perhaps the final story in the collection, "Something Falls," which was originally published in the Fall 1992 issue of *Ploughshares,* edited by Tobias Wolff, best exemplifies Treadway's prodigious skills as a writer. A law student reports she has been raped, but it is slowly revealed that the actual assault occurred many years before, that she had been abused by her father. Surprisingly, Treadway tells the story through the father's point of view, and it becomes impossible, as much as one resists, not to feel some empathy for him. Treadway does not ask her readers to forgive the father, but we begin to understand him. Throughout *Absent Without Leave,* Treadway compels us to look at all of her characters in the same light—allowing for the common, fatal flaw of being human.

Treadway, who currently teaches creative writing at Emerson College and is a Fiction Fellow at Radcliffe College's Bunting Institute, is at work on a novel, *Shirley Wants Her Nickel Back.* The novel expands on another story in her collection, "And Give You Peace," which was based on an incident in her hometown: a man shot his teenaged daughter to death, then killed himself, leaving his wife and two other daughters to wonder why. Treadway, who knew the three popular sisters, was shocked by the murder-suicide, and has always wondered how anyone could survive such a tragedy. She is about halfway through the novel.

The Zacharis First Book Award was inaugurated in 1991, when David Wong Louie was the winner for his short story collection, *The Pangs of Love*. Last year, Allison Joseph was honored for her poetry collection, *What Keeps Us Here*. The award is nominated by the Advisory Editors of *Ploughshares*, with Executive Director DeWitt Henry acting as the final judge. There is no application process.

Copies of *Ploughshares* Fall 1992, which includes Treadway's story "Something Falls" (then called "Down in the Valley"), are available for $6.00, postpaid.

NOTE TO OUR SUBSCRIBERS You might have noticed that we have been publishing *Ploughshares* a few weeks ahead of schedule with each issue this year. Our regular publication schedule is now April, August, and December. Copies will usually be mailed by our printer in North Carolina by mid-month, and delivery by domestic third-class mail takes anywhere from five to seventeen business days. However, estimates for "not delivered" third-class mail range from 3.5 to 7.4 percent, due to error, loss, damage, or theft. If you haven't received your copy of *Ploughshares* by the middle of May, September, and January, send us a postcard or give us a call. We'll gladly mail you another copy. But remember, the post office is not at fault when you move and do not notify us, since, as a policy, they do not forward magazines. Please try to inform us as soon as possible of address changes.

Please note, too, that on occasion we exchange mailing lists with other literary magazines. If you would like your name excluded from these swaps, just let us know.

INDEX TO VOLUME XIX

Ploughshares · A Journal of New Writing · 1993

Last Name, First Name, Title, Volume/Issue/Page

NONFICTION

BOOKSHELF

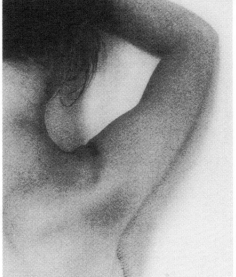

SUBMISSION POLICIES

Ploughshares · Winter 1993-94

Ploughshares is published three times a year: usually one fiction issue and two mixed issues of poetry and fiction. Each is guest-edited by a different writer, who will often be interested in specific themes or aesthetics. Postmark submissions to *Ploughshares*, Emerson College, 100 Beacon St., Boston, MA 02116-1596, between August 1 and April 1 (returned unread during April, May, June, and July). The Spring 1994 issue, poetry and fiction edited by James Welch, is editorially complete. Rosellen Brown, editor of our Fall 1994 issue, "invites personal essays on any subject—intimate memoir, scientific observation, cultural criticism, historical speculation, biographical recreation of figures great or small, public or private. The work may consist of narrative that reads like fiction; fragmented observation held together by the surface tension of theme and personality; travel writing that transcends tourist-diary notation; polemics that transcend propaganda. Only the kind of academic neutrality that banishes the personal voice will have a hard time. Writers are challenged to send work that enlarges private concerns into public questions or gives such immediacy of tone to public occupations that it makes them private and inescapable." You may call the *Ploughshares* answering machine, 617-578-8753, *after* 8 p.m., E.S.T., for guidelines of other issues as they are updated. We usually read from August to November for the Spring issue, from November to February for the Fall issue, and from December to March for the Winter issue. You may submit for a preferred issue, but please be timely, as we accumulate a backlog. All manuscripts must first be screened at our office; never send directly to a guest editor. Staff editors ultimately determine for which issue/editor a work is most appropriate. If an issue closes, the work is considered for the next one(s). Overall, we look for submissions of serious literary value. For prose, one story, memoir, or personal essay. No criticism or book reviews. Thirty-page maximum length. Typed double-spaced on one side of the page. For poetry, limit of 3-5 poems. Individually typed either single- or double-spaced on one side of the page. ("Phone-a-Poem," 617-578-8754, is by invitation only.) Always mail prose and poetry separately. *Only one submission of prose and/or poetry at a time, please.* Do not send another manuscript until you hear about the first. Additional submissions will be returned unread. Please mail your manuscript in a page-sized manila envelope, your full name and address written on the outside, to the Fiction, Nonfiction, or Poetry Editor. All manuscripts and correspondence regarding submissions should be accompanied by a self-addressed, stamped envelope (S.A.S.E.) for reply or return of manuscript, or we will not respond. Expect three to five months for a decision. Please wait five months to query us, then write, rather than call, indicating the postmark date of your submission. Simultaneous submissions are permitted. *We cannot accommodate revisions, changes of return address, or forgotten S.A.S.E.'s after the fact.* We cannot be responsible for delay, loss, or damage. We do not reprint previously published work. Payment is upon publication: $10 per printed page ($20 minimum, no maximum), with two copies of the issue and a one-year subscription.

Be an Expatriate Writer for Two Weeks.

Join a group of selected writers this summer for intensive fiction workshops in an exotic Dutch castle. With only twenty-five or so other seminar members, guided by five distinguished instructors, these two weeks are meant to be intimate and productive. In the mornings, short-story writers attend workshops, and novelists are individually advised on strategies for structure and revision, with the aim of completing publishable manuscripts. The afternoons are dedicated to private writing sessions and tutorials, ensuring that you will leave with new or honed work, as well as with redefined writing objectives. The evenings are set aside for readings and round-tables. Both the short-story and novel tracks concentrate on the craft and technique of fiction, and consider the pragmatics of the literary market. The dynamics of the seminar are carefully planned to include both published writers and those who are in the early stages of promising careers. The seminar is accredited for four academic credits and priced affordably. Inquire early to reserve your spot in this Renaissance castle. CO-DIRECTORS: Robie Macauley and Alexandra Marshall. FACULTY: James Carroll, Pamela Painter, and Thomas E. Kennedy, with a guest writer and visiting editor to be announced.

Fifth Annual

Ploughshares International Fiction Writing Seminar

Castle Well
The Netherlands

August 15–26, 1994

Emerson College
European Center

❏ Send me more information on the seminar and an application.

Name

Address

Mail or fax to: David Griffin · Division of Continuing Education
Emerson College · 100 Beacon St. · Boston, MA 02116
TEL (617) 578-8567 · FAX (617) 578-8618

Eat, Drink & Be Literary.

HARVARD BOOK STORE
CAFE

Breakfast through Late Dinner
190 Newbury Street at Exeter, Boston • 536-0095